CW00840968

Alexander McCall Smith is the author of the bestselling No. 1 Ladies' Detective Agency series. He has written many books for young readers, including the acclaimed School Ship *Tobermory* adventures.

Iain McIntosh's illustrations have won awards in the worlds of advertising, design and publishing. He has illustrated many of Alexander McCall Smith's books.

YOUNG PRECIOUS

THE COLLECTED ADVENTURES

ILLUSTRATED BY IAIN McINTOSH

ALEXANDER McCALL SMITH

This omnibus edition first published in 2021 by
BC Books, an imprint of Birlinn Limited
West Newington House
10 Newington Road
Edinburgh
EH9 1QS

www.bcbooksforkids.co.uk

Precious and the Monkeys
Copyright © 2011 Alexander McCall Smith
Illustrations copyright © 2011 Iain McIntosh

Precious and the Mystery of Meerkat Hill
Copyright © 2012 Alexander McCall Smith
Illustrations copyright © 2012 Iain McIntosh

Precious and the Missing Lion
Copyright © 2013 Alexander McCall Smith
Illustrations copyright © 2013 Iain McIntosh

Precious and the Zebra Necklace
Copyright © 2015 Alexander McCall Smith
Illustrations copyright © 2015 Iain McIntosh

The right of Alexander McCall Smith to be identified as
the author of these works has been asserted by him in
accordance with Copyright, Designs and Patents Act 1988

ISBN: 978 1 78027 741 7

British Library Cataloguing-in-Publication Data
A catalogue record for this book is available
from the British Library

Omnibus compilation by Hewer Text (UK) Ltd

Printed and bound by PNB, Latvia

Contents

A MAP OF
BOTSWANA

PULA

OKAVANGO

KALAHARI
DESERT

Francistown •

BOTSWANA

0   miles   100

GABORONE •

INTRODUCTION

A number of years ago I went to live for a short time in a country called Botswana. This is a very beautiful country in Africa – a place famous for its great wild places and the animals that live in them. When I lived there, I remember thinking: it would be fun to write about this place some day.

And I did. A long time afterwards, I sat down one day and wrote a story about a lady called Precious Ramotswe, who lives in Botswana, and who starts a little business. People thought that she might start a small store or something like that, but instead she sets up a detective agency. A detective agency! What does she know about being a detective? The answer to that is nothing, but – and this is an important but – she has just the right talents for it. She is a born detective – which means that she is somebody who is naturally good at the work involved in being a detective.

She is not one of those police detectives who solve major crimes. No, she is a person who deals with the mysteries that ordinary people – just like you and me – may have in their lives. So if we think that somebody is not telling us the truth about something, then we may go to her and ask her to find out what is really going on. Or if we have lost something that is very important to us, we may ask her to find it. Such people are called private detectives.

I have now written quite a number of books about Precious Ramotswe and from time to time, people have asked me more about her life. One of the questions I have been asked is this: what was Precious like as a girl? That is what these stories are about.

Although there is no actual Precious Ramotswe in real life, I can promise you that there are plenty of girls and women in Botswana who are just like her. I have met lots of ladies – and girls too – in that country who are every bit as intelligent and kind and nice as Precious Ramotswe is. And Botswana is real, as is the village of Mochudi, which is where she lives. So yes, it could be true – she really could exist.

That's enough from me. Now listen to the stories. Think of Africa. Think of a girl living there. Think of what it would be like to discover, when you are still quite young, that you are a born detective ...

ALEXANDER McCALL SMITH

Alexander McCall Smith

Precious and the Monkeys

HAVE YOU EVER SAID TO YOURSELF – not out loud, of course, but silently, just in your head: *Wouldn't it be nice to be a detective?* I have, and so have a lot of other people, although most of us will never have the chance to make our dream come true. Detectives, you see, are born that way. Right from the beginning, they just *know* that this is what they want to be. And right from the beginning, even when they are very young – a lot younger than you – they show that solving mysteries is something they can do rather well.

This is the story of a girl who became a detective. Her first name was Precious, and her second name was Ramotswe.

RAM•OTS•WE

That is an African name, and it is not as hard to say it as it looks. You just say RAM and then you say OTS (like *lots* without the l) and then you finish it off by saying WE. That's it.

This is a picture of Precious when she was about seven. She is smiling because she was thinking at the time of something funny, although she often smiled even when she was not thinking about anything in particular. Nice people smile a lot, and Precious Ramotswe was one of the nicest girls in Botswana. Everyone said that.

Botswana was the country she lived in. It was down towards the bottom of Africa, right in the middle. This meant that it was very far from the sea. Precious had never seen the sea, although she had heard people talk about it.

"The sound of the waves is like the sound of a high wind in the branches of the trees," people said. "It's like that sound, but it never stops."

She would have loved to stand beside the sea, and to let the waves wash over her toes, but it was too far away for her wish to be granted. So she had to content herself with the wide dry land that she lived in, which had a lot of amazing things to see anyway.

There was the Kalahari Desert, a great stretch of dry grass and thorn trees that went on and on into the distance, further than any eye can see. Then there was the great river in the north, which flowed the wrong way, not into the ocean, as rivers usually do, but back into the heart of Africa. When it reached the sands of the Kalahari, it drained away, just like water disappears down the plughole of a bath.

But most exciting, of course, were the wild animals. There were many of these in Botswana: lions, elephants, leopards, ostriches, monkeys – the list goes on and on. Precious had not seen all of these animals, but she had heard about most of them. Her father, a kind man whose name was Obed, had often spoken about them, and she loved the tales he told.

"Tell me about the time you were nearly eaten by a lion," she would ask. And Obed, who had told her that story perhaps a hundred times before, would tell her again. And it was every bit as exciting each time he told it.

"I was quite young then," he began.

"How young?" asked Precious.

"About eighteen, I think," he said. "It was just before I went off to work in the gold mines. I went up north to see my uncle, who lived way out in the bush, very far from everywhere."

"Did anybody else live there?" asked Precious. She was always asking questions, which was a sign that she might become a detective later on. Many people who ask lots of questions become detectives, because that is what detectives have to do.

"It was a very small village," said Obed. "It was just a few huts, really, and a fenced place where they kept the cattle. They had this fence, you see, which protected the cattle from the lions at night."

As you can imagine, this fence had to be quite strong. You cannot keep lions out with a fence that is no more than a few strands of wire. That is hopeless when it comes to lions – they would just knock down such a fence with a single blow of their paw. A proper lion fence has to be made of strong poles, from the trunks of trees just like the one below.

That is a good, solid lion fence.

"So there I was," Obed went on. "I had gone to spend a few days with my uncle and his family. They were good to me and I enjoyed being with my cousins, whom I had not seen for a long time. There were six of them – four boys and two girls. We had many adventures together.

"I slept in one of the huts with three of the boys. We did not have proper beds in those days – we had sleeping mats, made out of reeds, which we laid out on the floor of the hut. They were very comfortable, even if it doesn't sound like it, and they were much cooler than a bed and blankets in the hot weather, and easier to store too."

Precious was quiet now. This was the part of the story that she was waiting for.

"And then," her father continued, "and then one night I woke up to hear a strange sound outside. It was a sort of grunting sound, a little bit like the sound a large pig will make when it's sniffing about for food, only deeper."

11

"Did you know what it was?" she asked, holding her breath as she waited for her father to reply. She knew what the answer would be, of course, as she had heard the story so many times, but it was always exciting, always enough to keep you sitting on the very edge of your seat.

He shook his head. "No, I didn't. And that was why I thought I should go outside and find out."

Precious closed her eyes tight, just like this. She could hardly bear to hear what was coming.

"It was a lion," said her father. "And he was right outside the hut, standing there, looking at me in the night from underneath his great, dark mane."

Like this.

Precious opened her eyes cautiously, one at a time, just in case there was a lion in the room. But there was just her father, telling his story.

"How did that lion get in?" she asked. "How did he get past that big strong fence?"

Obed shook his head. "I later found out that somebody had not fastened the gate properly," he said. "It was carelessness."

But enough of that. It was time to get on with the story of what happened next.

WHAT WOULD YOU DO if you found yourself face to face with a great lion? Stand perfectly still? Turn on your heels and run? Creep quietly away? Perhaps you would just close your eyes and hope that you were dreaming – which is what Obed did at first when he saw the terrifying lion staring straight at him. But when he opened his eyes again, the lion was still there, and worse still, was beginning to open his great mouth.

Precious caught her breath. "Did you see his teeth?" she asked.

Obed nodded. "The moonlight was very bright," he said. "His teeth were white and as sharp as great needles."

Precious shuddered at the thought, and listened intently as her father explained what happened next.

Obed moved his head very slowly – not enough to alarm the lion, but just enough for him to look for escape routes. He could not get back to the hut, he thought, as it would take him too close to the frightening beast. Off to his left, though, just a few paces away, were the family's grain bins. These were large bins, rather like garden pots – but much bigger – that were used for storing the maize that the family grew for their food. They were made out of pressed mud, baked hard by the hot sun, and were very strong.

Obed lowered his voice. "I looked up at the night sky and thought, *I'll never see the sun again.* And then I looked down at the ground and thought, *I'll never feel my beloved Botswana under my feet again.* But the next thing I said to myself was, *No, I must do something. I must not let this lion eat me!*

"I made up my mind and ran – not back to the hut, but to the nearest grain bin. I pushed the cover back and jumped in, bringing the lid down on top of my head. I was safe!"

Precious breathed a sigh of relief. But she knew that there was more to come.

"There was very little grain left in that bin," Obed went on. "There were just a few husks and dusty bits. So there was plenty of room for me to crouch down."

"And spiders too?" asked Precious, with a shudder.

"There are always spiders in grain bins," said Obed. "But it wasn't spiders I was worried about."

"It was …"

Obed finished the sentence for her. "Yes, it was the lion. He had been a bit surprised when I jumped into the bin, and now I could hear him outside, scratching and snuffling at the lid.

"I knew that it would only be a matter of time before he pushed the lid off with one of his great paws, and I knew that I had to do something. But what could I do?"

Precious knew the answer. "You could take some of the dusty bits and pieces from the bottom of the bin and …"

Obed laughed. "Exactly. And that's what I did. I took a handful of those dusty husks and then, pushing up the lid a tiny bit, I tossed them straight into the face of the inquisitive lion."

Precious looked at her father wide-eyed. She knew that this was the good part of the story.

"And what did he do?" she asked.

Obed smiled. "He was very surprised," he said. "He breathed them in and then he gave the loudest, most amazing, most powerful sneeze that has ever been sneezed in Botswana, or possibly in all Africa. Ka… chow! Like this.

"It was a very great
sneeze," Obed said. "It was
a sneeze that was heard from
miles away, and it was certainly
heard by everybody in the village. In
every hut, people awoke, rubbed their
eyes, and rose from their sleeping mats.
'A great lion has sneezed,' they said to
one another. 'We must all hit our pots and
pans as hard as we can. That will frighten
him away.' "

And that is what happened. As the people began to strike their pots and pans with spoons and forks and anything else that came to hand, the lion tucked his tail between his legs and ran off into the bush. He was not frightened of eating one unfortunate young man, but even he could not stand up to a whole village of people all making a terrible din. Lions do not usually like that sort of thing, and this one certainly did not.

"I am glad that you were not eaten by that lion," said Precious.

"And so am I," said Obed.

"Because if the lion had eaten you, I would never have been born," Precious said.

"And if you had never been born, then I would never have been able to get to know the brightest and nicest girl in all Botswana," said her father.

Precious thought for a moment. "So it would have been a bad thing for both of us," she said at last.

"Yes," said Obed. "And maybe a bad thing for the lion too."

"Oh, why was that?"

"Because I might have given him indigestion," said Obed. "It's a well-known fact that if a lion eats a person who's feeling cross at the time, he gets indigestion."

Precious looked at her father suspiciously. She was not sure whether this was true, or whether he was just making it up to amuse her. She decided that it was not true, and told him so.

He smiled, and looked at her in a curious way. "You can tell when people are making things up, can't you?"

Precious nodded. She thought that was probably right – she *could* tell.

"Perhaps you should become a detective one day," he said.

And that was how the idea of becoming a detective was first planted in the mind of Precious Ramotswe, who was still only seven, but who was about to embark on a career as Botswana's greatest detective!

ETECTIVES sometimes say to one another: it's your first case that's always the hardest. Well, Precious was never sure if that was true for her, but her first case was certainly not easy.

It happened not long after her father had told her that one day she might become a detective. When he said that, she had at first thought *What a strange idea*, but then she asked herself, *Why not?* That's often what you think after somebody makes an odd suggestion. *Why not?* And after you've asked that question, you think *Well, yes!* And then you decide that there really is no reason why you shouldn't do it.

Not always, of course. If somebody suggests something stupid, or unkind, then you should quickly see all the reasons why not. And then you say, *No thank you!* Or *Certainly not!* Or something of that sort.

But Precious said to herself, "Yes, I could be a detective. But surely it will be years and years before I get a case."

She was wrong about that. A case came up sooner than she thought. This is what happened.

The school Precious went to was on a hill. This meant that children had quite a climb in the mornings, but once they were up there, what a wonderful place it was for their lessons. Looking out of the windows, they could gaze out to where other little hills popped up like islands in the sea. And you could hear sounds from far away too – the tinkling of cattle bells, the rumbling of thunder in the distance, the cry of a bird of prey soaring in the wind.

It was, as you can imagine, a very happy school. The teachers were happy to be working in such a nice town, the children

were happy to have kind teachers who did not shout at them too much, and even the school cat, who had a comfortable den outside, was happy with the mice that could be chased most days.

But then something nasty happened. That is what the world is sometimes like: everything seems fine, and then something happens to spoil things.

What happened was that there was a thief. Now, most people don't steal things. Most people – and that certainly includes you and me – know that things that belong to other people belong to other people. For many of us, that is Rule Number One, and sometimes you see it written out like this:

RULE NUMBER ONE
Don't help yourself to other people's things!

And Rule Number Two? Well that's another matter altogether, and we all know what it is anyway. So, a thief ... and a thief at school too!

The first person to notice what was going on was Tapiwa (TAP-EE-WAH) a girl in the same class as Precious.

TAP•EE•WAH

"Do you know what?" she whispered to Precious as they made their way home after school one afternoon.

"No," said Precious. "What?"

"There must be a thief at school," said Tapiwa, looking over her shoulder in case anybody heard what she had to say. "I brought a piece of cake to school with me this morning. I left it in my bag in the corridor outside the classroom." She paused before she went on. "I was really looking forward to eating it at break-time."

"I love cake," said Precious, closing her eyes and thinking of some of the cakes she had enjoyed. Iced cakes. Cakes with jam on top of them. Cakes sprinkled with sugar and then dipped in little coloured sugar-balls. There were so many cakes ... and all of them were so delicious.

"Somebody took my cake," Tapiwa complained. "I had wrapped it in a small piece of paper. Well, it was gone, and I found the paper lying on the floor."

Precious frowned. "Gone?"

"Eaten up," said Tapiwa. "There were crumbs on the floor and little bits of icing. I picked them up and tasted them. I could tell that they came from my cake."

"Did you tell the teacher?" asked Precious.

Her friend sighed. "Yes," she said. "But I don't think that she believed me. She said, 'Are you sure you didn't forget that you ate it?' She said that this sometimes happened. People ate a piece of cake and then forgot that they had done so."

Precious gazed at Tapiwa. Was she the sort of person to eat a piece of cake and then forget all about it? She did not think so.

"It was stolen," said Tapiwa. "That's what happened. There's a thief in the school. Who do you think it is?"

"I don't know," said Precious. She found it hard to imagine any member of their class doing something like that. Everybody seemed so honest. And yet, when you came to think of it, if there were grown-up thieves, then those thieves must have been children once, and perhaps they were already thieves even when they were young. Or did people only become thieves a bit later on, when they turned sixteen or something like that? It was a very interesting question, and she would have to think about it a bit more. Which is what she did as she walked home that day, under that high, hot African sun. She thought about thieves and what to do about them.

I T MIGHT HAVE BEEN EASY for her to forget about it – after all, it was only a piece of cake – but the next day it happened again. This time it was a piece of bread that was stolen – not an ordinary piece of bread, though: this one was covered in delicious red jam. You can lose a plain piece of bread and not think twice about it, but when you lose one spread thickly with red jam it's an altogether more serious matter.

The owner of this piece of bread (with jam) was a small boy called Sepo. Everybody liked this boy because he had a habit of saying funny things. And people like that, because there are enough sad things in the world as it is. If somebody can say something funny, then that often makes everybody feel a bit better. Try it yourself: say something funny and see how pleased everybody is.

This is a picture of Sepo.

You will see that he is smiling. And this is a picture of the piece of bread and red jam. Yes, if you saw such

a piece of bread sitting on a plate your mouth would surely begin to water. And yes, you might imagine how delicious it would taste. But would you really eat it if you knew it belonged to somebody else?

Of course not.

It happened at lunch-time. Every day, at twelve o'clock precisely, the school cook, a very large lady called Mma Molipi (MO-

MO•LEE•PEE

LEE -PEE), always called Big Mma Molipi, would bang a saucepan with a ladle. This was the signal for all the children to sit down on the verandah and wait to be given a plate of food that she had cooked with her assistant and cousin. This assistant was called Not-so-Big Mma Molipi, and,

as the name tells us, she was much smaller than the chief cook herself. This is a picture of the two of them standing together. You will see how different they are.

"Time for lunch!" Big Mma Molipi would shout in her very loud voice.

Then Not-so-Big Mma Molipi would shout, in a much smaller, squeakier voice, "Time for lunch!"

Big Mma Molipi's food was all right, but not all that all right. It was, in fact, a bit boring, as she only had one recipe, it seemed, which was a sort of paste made out of corn and served with green peas and mashed turnips.

Dinner time!

"It's very healthy," said Big Mma Molipi. "So stop complaining, children, and eat up!"

"Yes," said Not-so-Big Mma Molipi. "So stop complaining, children, and eat up!"

As you can see, Not-so-Big Mma Molipi did not say anything other than what she heard her larger cousin say. She thought it was safer that way. If you said anything new, she imagined, then people could look at you, and Not-so-Big Mma Molipi did not like the thought of that.

It was no surprise that many of the children liked to make lunch a little bit more interesting by bringing their own food. Some brought a bit of fruit, or a sugar doughnut, or perhaps a sweet biscuit.

Then, after lunch, when they all had a bit of free time before going back into the classroom, they would eat these special treats. Or, if they had nothing to bring, they could watch other people eating theirs. Sometimes, when you are very hungry, it's the next best thing just to watch other people eating. But this can also make you even hungrier, unless you are careful.

Sepo had brought his piece of bread and jam in a brown paper bag. While Big Mma Molipi served lunch, he had left the bag in

the classroom, tucked away safely under his desk. He was sure that this is where he left it, and so when he went back in and saw that it had disappeared he was very surprised indeed.

"My bread!" he wailed. "Somebody's taken my bread!"

Precious was walking past the open door of the classroom when she heard this. She looked in; there was Sepo standing miserably by his desk.

"Are you sure?" Precious asked.

"Of course I'm sure," said Sepo. "It was there when we went out for lunch. Now it isn't, and I didn't take it."

Precious went into the classroom and stared at the spot being pointed out by Sepo. There was certainly nothing there.

"I'll ask people if they saw anything," she said. "In the meantime, you can have half of my biscuit. I hope that will make you feel better."

It did. Sepo was still upset, but not quite as upset as he had been when he made the discovery.

"There must be a thief in the school," said Sepo as they walked out into the playground. "Who do you think it is, Precious?"

Precious shrugged. "I just don't know," she said. "It could be …" She paused. "It could be anyone."

Sepo looked thoughtful. "I think I may know who it is," he said. He did not speak very loudly, even though there was nobody else about.

Precious looked at him quizzically. "How do you know that? Did you see somebody taking it?"

Sepo looked furtively over his shoulder. "No," he said. "I didn't see anybody actually take it. But I did see somebody walking away from the classroom door."

Precious held her breath, waiting for

Sepo to say more. He stayed silent, though, and so she whispered to him, "Who?"

Sepo did not say anything, but after hesitating for a moment or two he very carefully pointed to somebody standing in the playground.

"Him," he whispered. "It's him. I saw him."

Precious frowned. "Are you sure?" she asked.

Sepo thought for a moment. If you ask somebody what they saw, they often have to think for a while before they answer. And they often get it wrong. But now Sepo said, "I'm sure – I really am. And look at him. Don't you think that he *looks* as if he's been eating too much!"

"Don't say anything," said Precious. "You can't accuse another person of doing something unless you actually saw it happen."

Sepo looked doubtful. "Why not?" he asked.

"Because you could be wrong," said Precious.

"But I'm not," said Sepo.

THAT NIGHT, as Precious lay on her sleeping mat, waiting for her father to come in and tell her a story – as he always did – she thought about what had happened at school. She did not like the thought of there being a thief at school – thieves spoiled everything: they made people suspicious of one another, which was not a good thing at all. People should be able to trust other people, without worrying about whether they would steal their possessions.

But even if she did not like the thought of there being a thief, neither did she like the thought that an innocent person might be suspected. She did not know the boy whom

Sepo had pointed out – she had seen him, of course, and she knew his name, Poloko (PO-LOW-KO), but she did not know very

PO◆LOW◆KO

much about him. And she certainly did not know that he was a thief.

This is Poloko.

You'll see that he was a rather round boy. If you saw him walking along the street, you might think that perhaps that was a boy who ate a little bit too much. And if you got to know him a bit better, then you might be sure that this was so and that those bulges in his pockets were indeed sweets – a large number of them. But just because somebody has lots of sweets does *not* mean 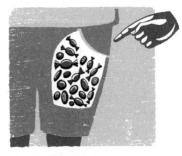 that he has stolen them. One thing, you see, does not always lead to another. That is something that all detectives learn very early in their career, and Precious had already learned it. And she was only seven.

The next day at school, when they were copying out letters from the board, Sepo, who was sitting on the bench next to Precious, whispered, "Have you told anybody about the thief?"

Precious shook her head. "We don't know who it is. How can I tell the teacher about something I don't know?"

Sepo looked cross. "But *I* know who it is," he said. "And Big Mma Molipi told me that somebody has stolen three iced buns from her kitchen! She told me that this morning. Poloko's probably eaten them already!"

Precious listened in silence. She thought it a very unfair thing to say and she was about to tell Sepo that when the teacher gave them a severe look. So Precious just said, "Shh!" instead and left it at that. But later, when the children were let out to play while the teachers drank their tea,

Sepo and Tapiwa came up to her and said they wanted to speak to her.

"Are you going to help us deal with the thief?" Tapiwa said.

Precious tried to look surprised. She knew what they meant, but she did not want to help them without any proof. "I don't know what you're talking about," she said. "How can we deal with the thief if we don't know who it is?"

"But we do know," said Sepo. "It's Poloko, that's who it is."

Precious stared at Sepo. "You don't know that," she said. "So I'm not going to help you until you have some proof."

Sepo smiled. "All right," he said. "If you want some proof, we'll get it for you. We're going to look at his hands."

Precious wondered what he meant by that, but before she had the time to ask him, Sepo and Tapiwa ran off to the other side of the playground where they had seen Poloko sitting on a rock. Precious ran behind them – not because she wanted to help them, but because she wanted to see what was happening.

"Hold out your hands," Tapiwa said to Poloko. "Come on. Hold them out."

Poloko was surprised, but held out his hands. Tapiwa bent down to examine them. After a few moments, she pointed out something to Sepo, and he also bent down to look. Then Tapiwa reached out to feel Poloko's hands.

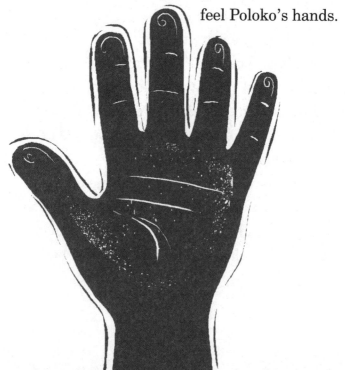

"Hah!" she shouted. "It's just as we thought. Your hands are sticky!"

Poloko tried to say something, but his words were drowned by the shouts of Tapiwa and Sepo. "Thief!" they cried out. "Thief! Thief!" It was a shrill cry, and it froze Precious's blood just to hear it. She wondered what it would be like to hear somebody shout that out about you – especially if you were not a thief and never had been.

Precious stood quite still.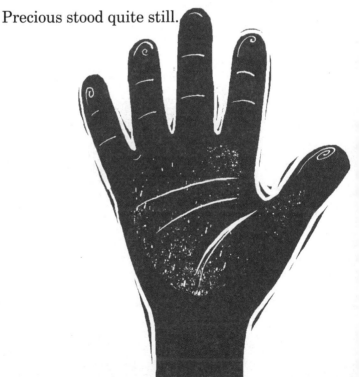

The others were now making such a noise that one of the teachers had been alerted and was coming to see what was wrong.

"What's all this noise?" the teacher asked. "Can't you children play quietly?"

"We've found the thief," Tapiwa shouted. "Look, Mma, look! His hands are covered in stickiness. If you want to know where those iced buns are, they're right there – in Poloko's stomach!"

THE TEACHER FROWNED. "What's all this?" she asked. "Are you children fighting?"

The two accusers were quick to deny this. "We're not fighting, Mma," cried Tapiwa, pointing a finger at Poloko. "We've found the thief. It's this boy! This boy right here!"

The teacher looked at Poloko. "Have you stolen something, Poloko?"

Poloko hung his head. "No, Mma, I have not stolen anything."

The teacher turned to stare at Tapiwa and Sepo. "Why do you say he's a thief?"

"Because some iced buns have been stolen," Sepo blurted out. "And his hands are sticky. Look at them, Mma!"

The teacher sighed. "Lots of people have sticky hands," she said. "That doesn't mean to say that they're thieves." She paused, looking down at Poloko. "You're sure you haven't stolen anything, Poloko?"

The boy was close to crying. "I have not stolen anything, Mma. I promise you."

The teacher shook a finger at Tapiwa and Sepo. "You be careful about accusing people of things when you have no proof," she said. "Now everybody go off and play and no more trouble, please."

Tapiwa and Sepo walked off, but only after throwing a disapproving look at Poloko. It was the sort of look that said *You're still a thief, you know.* And Poloko, who was clearly feeling very miserable, walked off in the other direction.

Precious waited for a moment before following the dejected-looking boy. "Poloko," she said, as she caught up with him. "I believe you. I don't think you're a thief."

He stopped. "Thank you, Precious. I know you don't think that." He paused, looking over his shoulder to where other children were standing, listening to Tapiwa and Sepo. "But they'll all think I'm a thief."

Precious knew that what he said was true. But she did not like to think that he was still unhappy, and so she tried to comfort him further. "It doesn't matter what people like that think," she said. "What matters is what your friends think. I'm your friend, and I know that you're telling the truth."

He listened to what she said and was about to say something when the bell sounded for them to return to the classroom. So he simply muttered "Thank you" and left it at that.

But Precious was not going to leave it there. That afternoon, when all the children left the school and began to walk back home under the hot African sun, she found Poloko and asked him to walk with her. They were going in the same direction, as he did not live far away from her.

He was pleased that she asked, as they could both see the other children looking at him suspiciously.

"You see," he said. "They've told everybody. Now they all think I'm a thief."

"Pay no attention to them," said Precious. "They can think what they like."

She knew, though, that it was not that simple. All of us worry about what other people think, even if we do not have to. It was easy to tell somebody to ignore that sort of thing; it was much harder to put such advice into practice.

They set off, following the path that wound down the hill. It was a narrow path and a winding one – here and there great boulders had rolled down the hill thousands of years ago and the path had to twist around these. In between the boulders, trees had grown up, their roots working their way through gaps in the stone. These trees made the places in between the rocks a cool refuge from the heat of the sun, and sometimes Precious would sit down there and rest on her way home. But these places were also good hiding places for snakes, and so you had to be careful or …

There was a noise off among the rocks, and they both gave a start.

"A snake?" whispered Poloko.

"Perhaps," said Precious. "Should we look?"

Poloko nodded. "Yes, but we must be careful."

They heard the noise again. This time Precious thought that it might be coming from the tree, and she looked up into the branches.

"There!" she said, pointing into the tangle of leaves.

Poloko looked up. He had expected to see a snake wound round one of the branches,

but that was not what he spotted.

"Monkeys!" he said.

Precious smiled. "They were watching us."

And then, just as she spoke, one of the monkeys dropped something. It fell down from the tree, caught in a shaft of light through the leaves. Poloko watched it, and then ran forward to pick it up, paying no heed to the excited chattering of the monkeys above his head.

For a moment or two he stared at it before passing it to Precious.

It was a piece of iced bun.

NOW SHE WAS SURE. But it was one thing to be sure about something and quite another to prove it to others. That was something that all detectives knew, and although she had only just started being a detective, Precious was well aware that you had to be able to show people something if you wanted them to believe it.

That night, as she lay on her sleeping mat, she went over in her mind what she had seen. The monkeys were the culprits – they had given themselves away – but it would not be easy to catch them in the act. Monkeys were very nimble, and, in their own, special monkeyish way, very cunning.

It was much easier to catch a human being red-handed than to catch a monkey.

Red-handed … It was just an expression, a couple of words that meant to catch somebody in the middle of doing something wrong, but it was a good way of putting it and … red-handed?

She closed her eyes and imagined how monkeys would steal buns. They would dart in through the window when nobody was looking and their little hands, so like human hands in every respect, but a bit hairier, would stretch out and snatch. Those little hands … What if the thing they were trying to snatch was even stickier than the stickiest of iced buns? What if it was a cake filled with … icing sugar and GLUE?

Like all good ideas, it was enough to make you sit bolt upright. And that is what Precious did, sitting up on her sleeping mat, her eyes wide, a broad smile on her

face. Yes! She had worked out how to trap a thief, particularly one with tiny hands!

She lay down and closed her eyes again. It took some time for her to drop off, as it often does when one has had a particularly clever idea, but eventually she became drowsier and drowsier and went off to sleep.

She dreamed, and of course her dreams were about monkeys. She was walking under some trees in her dream and the monkeys were up in the branches above her. They were calling out, and to her

surprise they were calling her name. *Come up here, Precious. Come up here and join us.*

In your dreams you can often do things that you just cannot do when you are awake. Precious could not normally climb trees very well, but in her dream she could. It was very easy, in fact, and within moments she was up in the branches with the monkeys. They gathered about her, their tiny, wizened faces filled with joy at finding a new friend. Soft, tiny hands touched her, stroking her gently, while other hands explored her ears and hair.

Then they took her by the hand and led her along one of the branches. The ground was far away below, so hard and rocky if you should fall. *Don't be frightened*, said one of the monkeys. *It's very easy, you know.*

And with that, Precious began to swing from branch to branch, just as the

monkeys do. It was the most wonderful, light feeling, and her heart soared as she moved effortlessly through the canopy of leaves. So this was what it was like to live in the trees – it was like living in the sky. And it was like flying too. As she let go of one branch and swung through the air to another, she felt as light as one of the leaves itself might feel as it dropped from the bough.

She moved through the trees, the monkeys all about her, waving to her, encouraging her. And then slowly the trees thinned out and she was on the ground again. She looked for her friends, the monkeys, and saw that they were gone. So it is with dreams: they take us to places we cannot stay; they bring us friends who will soon be gone. That is the way it is with dreams.

THE NEXT MORNING, Precious was the first in the house to get out of bed. She had work to do – detective work – and her first task was to bake a cake. This was not difficult, as she was a good cook and had a well-tried recipe for sponge cake. Precious had learned to cook because she had to – her mother had died when she was very small and although her father thought that he was looking after her, when it came to cooking meals it was Precious who looked after him!

The cake did not take long, and was soon out of the oven. It smelled delicious, but she resisted the temptation to cut a slice for herself and try it. Rather than do that, she took a knife and cut out the middle of the cake so that it was left with a large hole in it.

The next bit of the plan was more difficult. Her father had a workshop next to the house – a place where he fixed fence posts and did odd carpentry jobs for friends. On a shelf in this workshop was a large pot of glue that he used for sticking wood together – it was very strong glue, a thick, sticky paste that was just the thing she was looking for.

Very carefully, making sure to get none on her fingers, Precious ladled out several spoonfuls of this glue onto a plate. Replacing the glue-pot on the shelf, she went back to the kitchen. Now she took the piece of cake that she had cut from the centre and mixed it up with the glue. It made a wonderfully sticky mess – just what she wanted.

She next put this sticky mixture back into the hole in the cake and covered the whole thing with icing. For good measure, she stuck a few red and yellow jelly sweets on the top. Nobody would be able to resist such a cake, she thought. Certainly no monkey would.

"That's a nice cake you've cooked," said her father over breakfast. "Is that for your teacher?"

Precious smiled. "No, I don't think so." She could imagine what would happen if the teacher ate that particular cake.

"For your friends?" asked her father.

Precious thought for a moment. She remembered her dream and the way the monkeys in it had welcomed her to their trees. Yes, they were her friends, she thought. In spite of all their tricks and their mischievousness, they were her friends.

She carried the cake to school in a box. When she arrived, she put the box down carefully and took out its mouth-watering contents.

"Look at that cake!" shouted somebody.

"Don't leave it there," said another. "If you leave it there, Precious, then Poloko will be sure to steal it!"

Other children laughed at this, but Precious did not. "Don't say that," she said crossly. But they did, and they said it again.

"Poloko will eat that entirely up," said one of the boys. "That's why he's so fat. He's a fat thief!"

Precious hoped that Poloko had not heard this, but feared that he had. She saw him walking away, his head lowered. People are so unkind, she thought. How would they like to be called a thief? Well, she would show them just how wrong they were.

With the cake left outside, on the shelf where the children left their bags, school began. Precious went into the classroom and tried to concentrate on the lesson that the teacher was giving, but it was not easy.

Her mind kept wandering, and she found herself imagining what was going on outside. The cake would be sitting there, the perfect temptation for any passing monkey, and it could only be a question of time before …

It happened suddenly. One moment everything was quiet, and the next there came a great squealing sound from outside. The squealing became louder and was soon a sort of howling sound, rather like the siren of a fire engine.

The teacher and the entire class looked up in astonishment.

"What on earth is going on?" asked the teacher. "Open the door, Sepo, and see what's happening."

The entire class took this as an invitation to go to the door, and they were soon all gathered round the open door and the windows too, peering out to see what was going on.

What was happening was that two monkeys were dancing up and down alongside the shelf, their hands stuck firmly in the mixture of glue and cake. Struggle as they might to free themselves, each time they withdrew a hand it came out with a long strand of glue that dragged it back in. They were thoroughly and completely stuck to the cake.

"See," shouted Precious in triumph. "There are the thieves, Mma. See there!"

The teacher laughed. "Well, well. So it's monkeys who have been up to no good. Well, well!"

The school gardener had been alerted to the sound of squealing, and he now appeared. Seizing the monkeys, he pulled them away from the cake, freeing them to scamper back to the trees not far away.

"Little rascals," he shouted, shaking a fist at them as they disappeared.

The teacher called everybody back to their desks. "We shall have to be more careful in future," she said. "Don't leave anything out to tempt those monkeys. That's the way to deal with that."

Precious said nothing.

Then the teacher continued. "And I hope that some of you have learned a lesson," she said. "Those who accused Poloko of being a thief may like to think about what they have just seen."

The teacher looked at Sepo and Tapiwa, who both looked down at the floor. Precious watched them. They had learned a lesson, she thought.

On the way back from school that day, Poloko came up to her and thanked her for what she had done. "You are a very kind girl," he said. "Thank you."

"That's all right," she said.

"You're going to be a very good detective one day," he went on. "Do you still want to be one?"

She thought for a moment. It was a good thing to be a detective. You could help people who needed help. You could fight injustice. You could make people happier – as Poloko now was.

"Yes," she said. "I think I do."

They walked on. In the trees not far away, there were some small eyes watching them from the leaves. The monkeys. Her friends.

Poloko walked back past her house, and Precious turned to him and said, "Would you like me to make a cake? We could eat it for our tea?"

He said he would, and while Precious baked the cake, he sat outside and sniffed the delicious smell wafting through the kitchen window.

Then the cake was ready, and they each had a large slice.

"Perfect," said Poloko. "First class, number one cake."

And that is when she thought *When I have a detective agency I'll call it the No. 1 Ladies' Detective Agency*.

Many years later, she did just that. Which shows something else: when you decide that you want to do something, really want to do it, then you can. You really can.

AFRICA AFRICA AFRICA AFRICA AFRICA AFRICA

Botswana

AFRICA AFRICA AFRICA AFRICA AFRICA AFRICA

Alexander McCall Smith

Precious and the Mystery of Meerkat Hill

THIS IS THE STORY of a girl called
Precious. It is also the story of a
boy whose name was Pontsho, and
of another girl who had a very long name.
Sometimes people who have a very long
name find it easier to shorten it. So this
other girl was called Teb. There is no room
here, I'm afraid, to give her full name, as
that would take up quite a few lines. So,
like everybody else, we'll call her Teb.

Precious's family name was Ramotswe,
which sounds like this – RAM – OT – SWEE.
There: try it yourself – it's not hard to say.
She lived in a country called Botswana,

which is in Africa. Botswana is very beautiful – it has wide plains that seem to go on and on as far as the eye can see, until they join the sky, which is high and empty. Sometimes, you know, when you look up at an empty sky, it seems as if it's singing. It is very odd, but that is how it seems.

There are hills that pop up on these plains. The hills look rather like islands, and the plains look a bit like the sea. Here is a picture of what that is like.

Precious lived with her father, Obed, in a small house outside a village. Obed was a good, kind man who wore a rather battered old hat. That hat was well-known in the village and even further afield.

"Here he comes!" people would say when they saw his hat in the distance. "Here comes Obed!"

On one occasion Obed lost his hat while walking home in the dark. A wind blew up and lifted it right off his head, and because there was no light he was unable to find it. The next day, when he went back to the place where he had lost the hat, there was still no sign of it. He searched and searched, but without success.

"You could buy a new one, Daddy," Precious suggested.

Obed shook his head. "A new hat is never as comfortable as an old one," he said. "And I loved that hat." He paused, looking up at his daughter. "It saved my life, you know."

Precious wondered how a hat could save your life. "Please tell me about that," she said. She loved her father's stories, especially when he told them at bedtime.

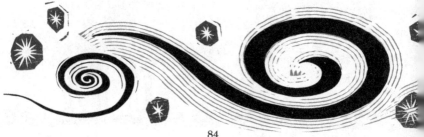

There is something very exciting about a bedtime story, and it is even better if the story is told after the lights have been turned out. The words sound different, I think – as if they are being whispered just for you and for nobody else. The words are all about you, like a warm blanket.

So Obed told her about the hat that evening, when it was already dark outside and the African sky was filling with stars.

"Quite a few years ago," he began, "before you were even born, I worked for a while on a farm. It was a very dry place, as there was not much rain in that part of the country. But each year the rains came, and the land would turn green as the plants returned

to life. That could happen so quickly – sometimes overnight.

"My job was to see that the cattle were getting water to drink. We had boreholes to pump the water up from deep wells. Then the cattle could slake their thirst from drinking troughs. I had to go and check that everything was working properly and fix it if it was not.

"Now, it was rather remote and empty down there, and although there were no lions, there were other wild animals – and birds. And this is all about one of those birds – a very dangerous bird."

Precious interrupted him. "Birds can't be dangerous," she said, laughing at the thought. "Birds are far too small."

Obed shook his head. "That's where you're wrong, my darling. There are some birds that are very big."

"An eagle?" asked Precious.

"Bigger than that. Much bigger."

She thought and thought, and was still thinking when Obed said: "An ostrich!

"An ostrich," her father went on, "is much bigger than a man, and yes, it can be very dangerous. You have to be very careful if you get too close to an ostrich because they can kick. They have these very strong legs you see, and at the end of one of them there is a claw. You can be very badly hurt by an ostrich kick – very, very badly hurt."

Precious shivered. Sometimes her father's stories were a little bit frightening, even if they usually ended well.

"Now," Obed continued, "I was walking through the bush one day, looking for some stray cattle, and suddenly I heard a noise. It was a very strange noise, and I stopped in my tracks wondering what it was. Then I saw it. Not far away from me, looking at me with those big angry eyes that they have, was an ostrich. And I knew right away that I had disturbed this creature and that it was about to attack me. The reason why it was so angry was that I had come too close to its nest. These birds make large nests on the ground in which they lay massive eggs. Think of a hen's

egg. Then think of an egg twenty times bigger than that – that's an ostrich egg.

"Suddenly I remembered something I had been told, and it was just as well it came back to me. Looking down on the ground, I saw a long stick that had fallen from a nearby tree. I picked this up and put my hat on the end of this stick. Then I held it up high in the air – like this.

"Ostriches may be strong, but they are not very bright. I had remembered being told that if you put your hat on a stick and then held it up high, an ostrich would think that the hat

was your head. They would also think that you were much taller than they were, and so they would leave you well alone. And, do you know, it worked! The ostrich saw my hat and thought I must be a very tall and strong creature – more than a match for her. So she backed off and I was able to continue on my way unkicked."

Precious breathed a sigh of relief. She did not want her father to be kicked by an ostrich – who does?

"I'm glad it worked out well for you," she said, as she drifted off to sleep.

"Thank you," said her father. "And now you go off to sleep, Precious, as you must be ready for school tomorrow morning."

Precious closed her eyes and thought of school. She had heard that there was a new family coming to the school the next day – a boy and a girl – and she wondered what they would be like. New people are always interesting, and she thought that perhaps they might be her friends. It was good, she thought, to have old friends, but it was also good to have new ones.

But what about the hat? Did Obed get it back after it had blown away? Yes, he did. It landed a long way away but when people picked it up they knew immediately whose it was, and it was returned to him a few days later none the worse for its adventure. Of course he was very pleased, and from that day onwards whenever there was a high wind, he held onto his hat very firmly. Which is what all of us should do, don't you think?

THE NEXT DAY Precious went to school eager to meet the two new arrivals. Neither of them was in her class, as one, the boy, was a year younger than she was, and his sister was a year older. But when the time came for the morning break, when the children spilled out of the classroom for half an hour of play, she quickly spotted them.

They were standing together under the shade of a tree. Precious noticed that they were watching the other children play, but not joining in. She understood that – she remembered what it was like to be new

to a school. Everybody else seems to know lots of people, and you know none. It is not at all easy.

She made her way through the jostling knots of boys and girls until she reached the tree.

"Hello," she said. "My name's Precious."

The girl smiled at her, and gave her their names. "I'm called Teb," she said. "And this is my brother, Pontsho."

Pontsho looked at Precious a little warily, but when he saw her smile he smiled back.

"You're new, aren't you?" said Precious.

"Yes," said the girl, glancing around her. "And I don't know anybody."

"Well," said Precious. "You know me now, don't you?"

The girl nodded.

"And I can tell you the names of everybody here," said Precious, looking around the group of children. "So I'm sure that you'll soon know everybody."

They talked until it was time to go back into the classroom. Even when she was a young girl, Precious was very curious to find out as much as she could about other people. That was why she became such a good detective when she grew up – detectives have to keep their eyes open; they have to look at people and think *I wonder who that person is. I wonder where he comes from. I wonder what his favourite colour is.* And so on. She was very good at all that.

But of course one of the best ways of finding something out is to ask somebody. That was a rule that Precious Ramotswe learned very early in her life, and never forgot. So that morning, as she stood under the tree and talked to Teb and Pontsho, she found out a great deal about the two newcomers just by asking a few questions.

For instance, she asked: "How many

people live in your house?"

And Teb replied: "There are six people who live in our house. There is me and my brother here – that's two. Then there's our mother, and our mother's sister. She is our aunt. And then there is our grandmother and our grandfather. They are very old. Our grandfather has no teeth left but our grandmother still has two or three. They

Grandmother's
TEETH

like to sit in the sun all day and watch what's going on. They are very kind to us."

And then Precious asked: "What about your father?"

This time the boy answered. "Our

father was struck by lightning two years ago," he said.

"That's very sad," said Precious.

The girl nodded. "And so we had to sell the place we lived in. We moved here because my grandfather had a small house that he owned. We all live in that now."

There were one or two other questions that Precious was able to ask. She asked how long it took them to walk to school, and they replied that it took just over half an hour. She asked them whether they believed in ghosts and Teb said no, although Pontsho hesitated a bit before he too said no. Then she asked them whether they liked apples, and Teb shook her head.

"I have never tasted an apple," she said. "Are they good?"

Precious tried not to show her surprise. Imagine never having tasted an apple! She herself loved apples, which her father bought her every Friday from one of the

village stores. And then she saw something that she had not noticed before. Neither of the children was wearing shoes.

It did not take her long to work things out. Teb and Pontsho must be very poor. That was why they had never tasted an apple and that was why they had no shoes. The thought made her sad. To walk to school for half an hour on ground that could become burning hot during the summer could not be easy. Of course your feet got used to it, and the skin underneath became harder and harder, but it must still have been uncomfortable. And what about thorns? Some of the bushes that grew at the side of paths were known for

their vicious thorns. It would be only too easy to get one of these in your foot, and she knew how painful that could be.

She did not say anything, though. Sometimes people who are very poor are ashamed of it, even if they have no reason to be. Being poor is usually not your fault, unless it's because you are very lazy. There are all sorts of reasons why people can be poor. They may have not been able to find any work. They may be in a job where they are not paid very much. They may have lost their father or mother because of illness or an accident or, Precious thought, lightning. Yes, lightning was the reason here, and it made her sad just to think of it.

The bell sounded for the end of the morning break. "We have to go inside now," said Precious. "But if you like, I can walk home with you and we can talk a bit more. Your house isn't far from mine."

"I would like that very much," said Teb. And then she added: "And if you come to my place, my brother can show you something really special." She turned to Pontsho and gave him a warning look. "But don't tell her yet, Pontsho! Let it be a surprise."

"I won't tell," said the boy. And smiled.

CHAPTER THREE

PRECIOUS could hardly contain her excitement on the walk to Teb's house. She wondered what her new friends could have in store for her, but try as she might, she could not guess what it was. That's the thing about a *real* surprise – you have no idea what it can possibly be, and the more you think about it, the harder it becomes to imagine what it is. Try it. Try to think of something that you don't know anything about. Hard, isn't it?

After they had been walking for a while Teb said: "We're just about there. Our house is just down there. See, near that hill? Where those trees are? That's our place."

They were now outside the village, and there were no other buildings to be seen. There were plenty of trees, though, and it took Precious a few moments to work out which trees Teb meant. But then she saw a wisp of smoke rising up into the sky and she knew that this was from somebody's cooking fire. And, sure enough, when her eye followed the smoke down she saw that there was a small house tucked away at the end of it. So that was Teb's place.

They followed the path that led to the house and soon they were there.

"This is our place," said Teb. "This is where we live."

Precious looked at the house. It was not very large and she wondered how everybody could fit inside. But she did not want to say anything about that, as people are usually proud of their houses and do

not like other people (and that means us) to point out that their houses are too small, or too uncomfortable, or the wrong shape.

And so she said, 'That's a nice house, Teb."

That was not a lie. It is not a lie to say something nice to somebody. You have to remember that you can usually find something good to say about anything if you look hard enough. And it's kind too,

and Precious Ramotswe was a kind girl, as everybody knew.

Teb beamed with pleasure. "Thank you," she said. "It's a bit small maybe, but then my brother sleeps out at the back, under a shelter, and so he doesn't take up much room. And my grandfather sleeps during the day and so he doesn't really need a bed at night – he just sits in his chair until morning. He's very happy, you know."

Precious looked about her. In front of the house she saw two chairs, and in those two chairs she suddenly noticed that there were two very old people, both wearing hats that had been pulled down over their eyes.

"That's my grandfather and grandmother," explained Teb. "You may think they can't see anything, with those hats pulled over their eyes, but they can. They have small holes in the hats, you see, and they see through those."

Precious looked again, and saw that what Teb said was right. There were small holes in the hats and through those holes she could just make out ... eyes.

And then one of the people raised a hand to wave to her, and then the other did the same thing. So Precious waved back.

Teb and Pontsho now took Precious to say hello to their grandparents. Precious did this, and was greeted very kindly.

"How do you do?" asked the grandfather. "You are very welcome. Thank you for coming. Good day."

And the grandmother said: "How are

you? It is very nice to see you. Good day too, my dear."

Then Teb took her into the kitchen, which was the first room that you went

into when you entered the front door. There she met Teb's mother and her aunt, who were both busy crushing grain in a large tub. Some people don't know that bread comes from grain. You do, of course, but others have to be told that not everybody can go into a shop and buy a loaf of bread. Some people don't have shops anywhere near them, and some don't have the money to buy bread. So they have to

Grain

make it. And it tastes delicious!

They went outside again, and it

was now that Precious learned what the big surprise was. And it was truly surprising. It was the sort of surprise that she would never have guessed, even if she had tried to do so for hours and hours.

What was this surprise? Well, here it is. It was a MEERKAT.

Now, what exactly is a meerkat? Well, it's not a cat. And it's not a squirrel, nor a racoon, nor a … Perhaps it's a mongoose, but it's easiest to think of them as being … just meerkats. They look like meerkats and they do the things that meerkats do – which is just what this meerkat now did, standing up on its hind legs, its front paws held out for balance, and its small black nose sniffing at the air with the greatest possible interest.

"A meerkat!" exclaimed Precious. "You've got a meerkat!"

Teb smiled. "Yes," she said. "This is Kosi. He belongs to my brother. His name means *chief*, you know."

Precious leaned forward and, as she did

so, the meerkat leaned forward too, his bright little eyes shining, his nose moist and glistening.

"He likes you," said Pontsho. "You can tell when he likes somebody."

"And I like him too," said Precious. "Can I touch him?"

"Of course," said Teb. "Be gentle, though, as he can sometimes be a bit frightened."

Precious reached forward and placed a finger as gently as she could on the back of the meerkat's head, as if to stroke him. His fur was smooth, a little bit like that of a well-groomed cat. It was a very strange feeling to be touching a meerkat.

Kosi half-turned his head when she touched him, but Precious could see that he was not in the least bit frightened.

"Where did you get him?" she asked.

Pontsho pointed to the hill behind the house.

"From the hill over there," he said. "I

think he must have been separated from the rest of his family. He was sitting on one of the rocks, looking very lost. We call it Meerkat Hill now, because of him."

"What does he eat?"

Pontsho smiled as he answered her question. "He likes insects," he said. "He loves worms. And he even likes to eat scorpions."

Precious made a face. "Scorpions!"

"Yes," said Teb. "He's very brave."

"Brave enough to face up to a snake," said Pontsho. "Even a cobra."

Precious drew in her breath. Cobras were very, very dangerous snakes and the

thought that such a tiny creature as this could stand up to that deadly snake was hard to believe.

"Tell her," said Teb. "Tell Precious about the cobra."

So they sat down, with Kosi sitting down beside them, as if he too was listening to the story that Pontsho then began.

"T HIS HAPPENED quite a long time ago," began Pontsho.

"Last month," said his sister, correcting him.

"Well, that's quite a long time ago," said the boy. "It didn't happen yesterday, did it?"

"It doesn't matter," said Precious. "I want to hear the story about the cobra. Just carry on with that."

Pontsho began again. "So," he said, "this happened quite a long time ago – last month. Our grandparents, as you know, like to sit in the sun. Sometimes they just sit and sleep, but sometimes they just sit. They've worked very hard all their lives, you see, and they're a bit tired now.

"Well, they were sitting there sleeping one afternoon. I had been off with Kosi to find some worms for his dinner that night. We found some very juicy-looking ones and his stomach was tight and full. He was very pleased with himself, I think.

"The moment I got back to the house, I noticed that something was wrong. Or at least I saw that something was different."

Pontsho paused now, and looked at Precious, who was following his story wide-eyed. "What was it?" she asked. "What did you see?"

"My grandfather has big feet," said Pontsho. "When he sleeps he likes to take his shoes off, and so he had no shoes on. And do you know what I saw? I saw that a great big snake had curled himself round my grandfather's toes! Snakes like to do that, you know. I think it keeps them warm. They love people's toes."

Precious gasped. She did not like the idea of having a snake curled around *her* toes. "Go on," she urged. "What happened next?"

"I wasn't sure what to do," said Pontsho. "For a little while I stood quite still with shock. You know how it is when you see something really frightening? You sometimes just stand there, unable to do anything. Well, that was how it was. And

I was so shocked I forgot that I had Kosi with me.

"He had seen the snake too. He had been sitting on my shoulder, as he often likes to do when we go for a walk together. Now he jumped down and began to move very slowly towards my grandparents. Do you know how a cat will move when it's stalking a bird? That was how he moved. Very, very slowly, and very quietly."

Precious drew in her breath. "Did the snake see him?" she asked.

"Not to begin with," answered Pontsho. "But as he began to get closer and closer, the snake started to move. It didn't move

its coils – it just moved its head, which had bright black eyes like little pinpoints of dark light. And it put out its tongue, which came out like a tiny wet fork and then went back in. That's how snakes smell things, you know – they stick out their tongue and then take the smell back inside.

"I was really worried," Pontsho continued. "If the snake became angry, then he could very easily bite my grandfather. And if that happened, then there would be very little we could do for him. A cobra injects poison through his fangs and it stops you breathing and makes your heart stop too. My grandfather would never wake up if that happened. It would be the end of him.

"But then something really amazing happened. Kosi began to scratch at the ground as if he was looking for a worm, or even a scorpion. I could hardly believe it. Why would he suddenly be hungry after eating all those juicy worms we had found? But then I understood what he was doing. He was attracting the attention of the snake.

"The snake moved his head again. He was watching the meerkat and he was clearly thinking: 'Now there's a tasty little creature that would go very nicely down my throat!' A big snake, like a cobra, loves to eat meerkats – if he can catch them.

"Very slowly, the cobra began to unwind himself from my grandfather's feet. Very smoothly, like a long piece of hosepipe, he moved across the ground towards Kosi.

I stood quite still, although I was terrified that Kosi was going to be caught by the snake. I love him so much, you know, and I would never find another meerkat if anything happened to him.

"The next thing I knew was that Kosi had jumped up in the air. This happened

at exactly the moment that the cobra struck at him. He missed, of course, and his fangs ended biting the ground rather than a meerkat arm or leg. Kosi was safe, and now he ran helter-skelter towards some thick grass with the snake sliding after him, its hood up in anger.

"Ten minutes later, Kosi came back

unharmed. He had led the snake off into the grass and left him there. The snake never returned."

"And what did your grandfather think?" asked Precious.

"He had been asleep all along," said Teb. "So he didn't mind. But he was very grateful to Kosi, of course. 'Take good care of that meerkat,' he said to Pontsho."

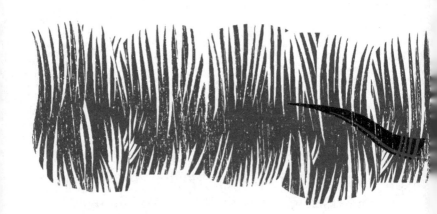

"And I do," said the boy. "I really do."

Precious smiled, and tickled the meerkat under his chin, just as she had seen Pontsho do. The tiny creature liked that, it seemed, closing his eyes with pleasure. He was so small, thought Precious, and yet he had been brave enough to lure away a fully grown cobra. Small and brave, she thought. Small and brave.

PRECIOUS thought a lot about Kosi over the next few days. Whenever she saw Pontsho at school she would ask him how the meerkat was, and he would tell her of Kosi's latest adventures. He had caught a large scorpion, he said, or he had stolen a piece of bread from the kitchen, or had done some other thing that meerkats like to do. One of these things, Pontsho told her, was to ride on the back of the family's cow. "He loves doing that," said Pontsho. "He sits on the cow's back for hours, looking out over everything. It's his favourite place, I think."

Precious smiled at this and said she

hoped that she would have the chance to see him again soon.

"Perhaps you will," said Pontsho, and winked.

She was to find out what that wink meant a few days later. Going outside during the morning break, she saw Pontsho beckoning her.

She went to join him. "Yes?" she said. "Did you want something, Pontsho?"

He drew her aside. "He's here," he whispered.

Precious was puzzled. "Who's here?"

"Your friend," said Pontsho, pointing to his school bag. "Kosi."

Precious looked down at the bag. To her astonishment, she saw a small nose sticking out of one corner, sniffing the air. Pontsho had brought Kosi to school.

She was excited, but at the same time she was more than a little bit worried. "You'll get into trouble," she warned.

Pontsho shook his head. "Nobody will find out," he said. "He wanted to come, you see. He'll be good."

No sooner had he said that than he was proved quite wrong. Somehow Kosi managed to get the top of the bag undone. Then, with a wiggle and a twist – the sort of movement that only meerkats can

manage – he was out of the bag. Precious gasped as the meerkat, looking about him with interest, thought about what to do next. And then she gasped again – more loudly this time – when the tiny creature decided to dash off across the playground and head straight for the one place she hoped he would not go: the teachers' room.

This room was beside the classrooms and it was where the teachers went to drink tea while the children played outside. Its door was always left open, so that the

teachers could see if anybody got up to mischief outside. But that meant that for a meerkat, looking around for somewhere to go, it seemed like a very good place to investigate.

As Kosi vanished into the teachers' room, Pontsho and Precious ran behind him, stopping short of the door itself, but standing where they could see what was happening inside. It was a very funny sight, but one that still made Precious and Pontsho hold their breath in alarm.

Entering the room, all that Kosi must have seen was legs – a whole forest of legs. Now for a meerkat, there is nothing more interesting than legs. From the meerkat point of view, legs are trees, and trees, as every meerkat knows, are for climbing up. That gives them a better view of what is happening in the long grass around them. Every meerkat is taught that and every meerkat remembers it.

Kosi made his way cautiously around the legs and ankles. Now and then he stopped, and would fiddle with a shoe-

lace or gingerly touch a bony ankle; now and then he would dodge out of the way if a foot was suddenly moved. But then, finding a pair of particularly stout legs, he stopped and looked up. These legs were clearly very interesting to him, and he appeared to be unsure as to whether or not to climb them. They looked very much like trees to Kosi – even if they were, in fact, the legs of the Principal of the school, a rather strict man who did not like it at all when anybody did something wrong.

"Oh no," groaned Pontsho, as he saw

what was happening.

Kosi took a step forward and took hold of the principal's trousers. Up above, the Principal felt something, and perhaps thought that a fly, or even maybe a spider, had landed on him and would need to be brushed off. He was busy talking to one of the teachers at the time, and so he just leant forward, without looking what he was doing, and brushed the fly away.

Kosi saw the Principal's hand approaching him and did what any meerkat would do. He leapt up as high as he could – and landed on the head of the teacher sitting next to the Principal. In nature, meerkats will always seek the highest or the lowest point when they are worried. The highest point gives them a good view of approaching danger, and the

134

lowest point gives them refuge.

The teacher screamed. She had no idea what was perched on the top of her head as she could not see what it was. But the other teachers could, and they all cried out.

"He's on your head!" they shouted.

And then they started to laugh. It was, of course, a very funny sight, and although we shouldn't laugh at people, there are times when it's impossible to keep the laughter in.

Happily, the teacher herself imagined how funny she must have looked, and began to laugh too.

Pontsho felt that there was only one thing to do. He knew that it would get him into trouble, but he had to retrieve Kosi from the teacher's head. So he stepped forward, into the teacher's room, and called Kosi to him.

Seeing Pontsho, Kosi straightaway jumped off the teacher's head and scampered across the room to his owner.

"Young man," said the Principal sternly, "you have a lot of explaining to do."

Pontsho said he was sorry. He knew that nobody was allowed to bring animals to school, and he would not do it again.

The Principal looked at him. He was frowning, and Pontsho knew that he was going to get into deep trouble. But then, quite suddenly, the Principal stopped frowning and a broad smile appeared on his face.

"Well," he said, "the rules say that nobody can bring a dog to school. They also say something about not bringing mice or other pets like that. But they don't say anything about meerkats, do they?"

"No," said one of the teachers, beginning to laugh. "They don't."

The Principal raised a finger. "That's

not to say that the rules won't say that in the future," he said. "But for today, I think it will be all right."

Pontsho looked at Precious with relief. She was standing at the door watching what was happening, and she was smiling too.

"You should tell us a bit more about this funny little creature," said the Principal. "Come on – don't be shy."

So Pontsho told the teachers all about Kosi and about how he had saved his grandfather. At the end of this tale, the teachers all crowded round and were allowed to pat Kosi gently on the head. Pontsho swelled with pride, as did Precious, and, I think, little Kosi

did too. Meerkats like attention. They like people to pat them on the head and say nice things. Rather like the rest of us, don't you think?

CHAPTER
SIX

KOSI'S visit to school ended well but then, a few days later, when school had just finished for the day and Precious was starting her walk home, she came across Teb sitting by the side of the road – and she was crying. There was no sign of Pontsho.

"What's wrong?" she asked, putting her arm around her friend's shoulder.

For a little while Teb was sobbing too much to answer, but then she turned to Precious and told her. "Our cow," she said, "is going to have a calf. But she wandered off yesterday and she hasn't come back. Pontsho stayed at home today to help call

her." Precious said she was very sorry to hear this news. She understood how important that cow was to Teb's family. It was just about everything they had. And when the calf was born that would be important too, as they could sell that to somebody and use the money to pay for food.

Teb dried her tears. "My mother doesn't know what to do," she said. "We've called her and called her, but we have no idea where she's gone. Sometimes cows do that, my grandfather said. He told me that cows just wander off and never return."

Precious thought hard. She had already decided, even at her age, that when she grew up she would be a detective, and now here was a case right in front of her that needed solving.

"Can I help?" she asked gently.

Teb turned to her. "Could you?" she asked.

"Yes," said Precious. But even as she spoke, she wondered what she could possibly do to solve the mystery of the missing cow. But, after a moment or two, it came to her. Had they looked for tracks? When cows walk on the ground, they leave hoof-prints where they have been. Had Teb or Pontsho looked for these?

Teb shook her head.

"Then we should do so," said Precious. "I'll come home with you now and we can start to look for tracks."

Teb immediately brightened. "My mother will be very pleased if we find her," she said. "She'll make us all a reward of fat cakes!"

Precious loved fat cakes, which are a delicious type of fried doughnut that are very popular in Botswana. But she did not like to think of a reward just yet. It was all very well having an idea, but as every detective knows only too well, not all ideas solve the case.

When they reached the house, Pontsho ran out to meet them. At first they thought he might be bringing good news, but when they saw his face, they realised that this was not so.

"We've called and called," he said hoarsely. "But we haven't found her."

Teb told him about the idea that Precious had come up with. Pontsho thought for a moment and then nodded. "Let's look," he said.

They led Precious to the place where the cow had last been seen. This was a small clearing at the bottom of Meerkat Hill,

right behind the family's house. There was a fence, but it was an old one, and it would have been very easy for a cow just to step over it if she really wanted to.

Precious started to walk round the fence, taking great care not to disturb the ground. Detectives always do that, as you probably know: they don't want to destroy any of the clues that may be lying around. And here was one, right in front of her.

"Over here," she called, pointing to the ground in front of her.

Teb and Pontsho ran over to join her.

"This is where she went," said Precious. "Look. There are the marks of her hooves."

Cow

Rock Rabbit

Elephant

Teb and Pontsho peered down at the tracks in the dusty soil.

"Now," said Precious. "If we follow them, we'll see where she went."

They set off, and everybody was very excited. So excited were they, in fact, that they did not notice that they had been joined by Kosi, who was following behind them, his little nose twitching with interest.

Fortunately it had not rained. Botswana is a dry country, and the rain only comes in what they call the rainy season – those

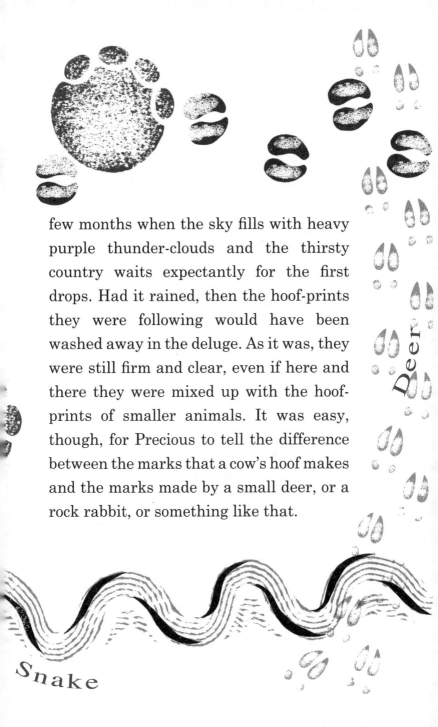

few months when the sky fills with heavy purple thunder-clouds and the thirsty country waits expectantly for the first drops. Had it rained, then the hoof-prints they were following would have been washed away in the deluge. As it was, they were still firm and clear, even if here and there they were mixed up with the hoof-prints of smaller animals. It was easy, though, for Precious to tell the difference between the marks that a cow's hoof makes and the marks made by a small deer, or a rock rabbit, or something like that.

Deer

Snake

Pontsho had now spotted Kosi and had invited him to travel on his shoulder. The meerkat liked that, and sat importantly on his vantage point, as if it was he who was the detective and not Precious Ramotswe. Well, as we will shortly find out, there was some truth in that, but for now here they are, all following the tracks, the heart of each of them filled with hope that they would soon find the missing cow.

THE COW had wandered a long way. At times, when she had crossed stony ground, the tracks became faint, and Precious had to get down on her hands and knees to see them. At other times, though, the cow had made her way over bare sandy soil, and the hoof-prints were very easily visible.

They had been walking for well over an hour and were beginning to wonder whether they would ever catch up with the cow when Pontsho suddenly called out.

"Over there!" he shouted. "Look!"

They stopped and stared in the direction

147

in which he was pointing. For a moment or two Precious could not make out what it was that had attracted the boy's attention, but then she saw it. A large herd of cattle was gathered beside a rough dirt road that ran through the scrub bush.

Pontsho whistled. "Look how many there are," he said. "I wonder what's going on."

Precious knew the answer to that. Her father knew a lot about cattle, and had once taken her to see a herd being prepared for market. This was what was happening here: a farmer had gathered

in all his cattle to be collected for market. Unfortunately the cow must have heard or smelled them and had decided to join them. After all, if you are a cow and you see lots of other cows getting together, you must think: why shouldn't I be there too?

The three children ran towards the herd. They had seen a couple of men standing nearby and they imagined that these were the people in charge. All they would have to do was to identify their cow and then lead her back to her home.

It was Teb who spoke first.

"Excuse me," she said very politely. "Our

cow has run away. We've tracked her and we think she's joined this herd. Could we have her back please?"

The two men, who had been talking to one another, stopped their conversation and looked at Teb.

"These are our cows," one said. "Sorry. Your cow must have gone somewhere else."

"No," said Precious. "She's here. We followed her hoof-prints."

One of the men laughed. "Followed her hoof-prints? What nonsense! These cows all belong to us."

Precious bit her lip. It was hard not to be believed when you know that you're telling the truth. But there is no point in getting cross about it, because that can only make it worse. So instead of insisting that she was right, she simply said to the men, "But if we could prove it? Would you let us take our cow?"

Both men nodded. "Of course," one said.
Then he added, "But I really don't see how
you're going to do that. All these cattle
look the same, you know."

With a sinking heart, Precious saw that
this was so – all the cows were more or less
the same colour – reddish-brown. But then,
without having to think about it, she had

an idea. It was the second good idea that had come to her that day, and she lost no time in explaining it to Teb and Pontsho.

"Listen," she said, dropping her voice so that the men could not hear her. "Do you think that Kosi would know your cow, even in a big herd?"

It was Pontsho who answered. "Of course," he said. "He loves to ride on her back, as I told you. They're very good friends."

This was the answer Precious had been hoping for. "Right," she said. "Let's ask him to find her."

Kosi frowned. "How will we do that?"

Precious looked at the meerkat, who was sitting on Pontsho's shoulder watching the restless herd of cows with interest. "Ask him," she said. "Meerkats are good at understanding things. He might be able to do it."

Then she turned to the men. "Excuse me," she said. "This meerkat knows my friends' cow very well. If he can find her, will you let us take her home?"

The men laughed. "Of course," said one of them. "Of course we'll let you take her home. But how is a tiny little meerkat

going to find one cow in a large herd like this? It won't happen, will it?"

Precious did not answer that question, but turned to Pontsho. "Ask him, Pontsho," she said.

Pontsho took Kosi off his shoulder and put him down on the ground. "Find your friend," he whispered. "Find her!"

The meerkat got up on its hind legs and looked at Pontsho enquiringly. Then he turned his nose towards the herd of cows and sniffed at the air. Precious held her breath. Was it possible that the meerkat understood what was expected of him?

And then, with a sudden little jump – a hop of the sort that meerkats perform when they have some task to do – Kosi scurried off into the herd, weaving and dodging to keep out of the way of the cows' hooves. From where Precious was standing, it looked very dangerous – and it was. At one point she thought that

Kosi would be crushed, but he proved too nimble for that, and managed to avoid being stamped upon.

When the meerkat reached the centre of the herd he seemed to disappear for a moment. But then he suddenly popped up again, and now he was riding on the back of one of the cows. "That's her!" shouted Teb. "See! That's her."

Precious turned to the men. "Do you see that?" she asked. "You wanted proof

– well there it is. The meerkat has found her friend."

The men may have been a bit gruff, but they were not ones to break their promise. They had said that if the meerkat found the cow, then the children could take her home. And so they set about rounding up Teb's cow, who still had a meerkat perched on her back.

"You can take her home, I suppose," said one of the men. And then, even if a

bit reluctantly, he added, "And well done, whoever it was who came up with that idea!"

Precious said nothing. She did not like to boast, and the fact that the family had recovered their cow was more than enough reward for her.

T HEY LED THE COW home, guiding her gently along the path they had followed to find her. When they reached the bottom of Meerkat Hill, Precious could see the two grandparents waving their hands excitedly. They were soon joined by Teb's mother and the aunt, both of whom joined in the energetic waving.

"This is a miracle," said the grandfather as he ran forwards to welcome the returning cow. He could not run very fast, as his legs were a bit bent and spindly, but he did his best, and was soon stroking the cow on the side of her neck, whispering

159

into her ear the sort of things people say
to cows who have been away but who have
come back.

"This is wonderful," said Teb's mother.
"I think you all deserve a reward for
finding our cow."

Teb glanced at Precious, and smiled.
Then she turned to her mother and asked,
"Fat cakes?"

Her mother nodded. "I shall make them
immediately, even if it's almost time for
our evening meal."

The mention of evening made Precious
look at the sun, which was now beginning

to drop down in the sky. "I'll have to get home soon," she said. "My father will be beginning to get worried."

Teb looked imploringly at her mother. "Can't Precious stay?" she asked.

"I could go and ask her father," said the aunt. "I have to go to the store, and I could call at their house and ask him if Precious can stay overnight."

Both Teb and Pontsho thought this was a very good idea, as did Precious herself of course, and the aunt lost no time in setting off on her mission. By the time the fat cakes were ready and sprinkled with sugar, the aunt had come back to announce that Obed had said that it was perfectly all right for his daughter to stay overnight at Teb's house.

They sat and ate the fat cakes. There were two each for everybody, which was more than enough, as the grandparents could not finish theirs and passed them on. The children kindly finished them for them, and then everybody licked their fingers to get the last of the sugar and stickiness off. The last bits of everything taste particularly good, don't you find?

By now it was beginning to get dark. The sun in Africa sinks rather quickly. The sky turns a coppery gold colour and then down beyond the horizon goes the great red ball of the sun. As soon as it is gone, the sky becomes light blue again and then dark blue, and the stars appear – great silver fields of them.

Since it was a special occasion, the

grandfather made a fire outside for Teb,
Pontsho and Precious to sit around. Then
he moved his chair to the fire too, and
told them a story of how things were a
long time ago, when he was a boy. They
listened, and then, after he had finished
and had moved his chair back to its usual
place, they talked among themselves.

There was much to talk about. They
remembered all about following the cow's
hoof-prints and Pontsho thought that
he would try his skill at tracking other

animals in future, now that Precious had shown him how to do it. Teb thought this was a good idea, and said that she would practise looking for clues, just as Precious had done. "You never know what you might find," she remarked. "There are all sorts of mysteries once you start to look for them."

Precious agreed. She had only been a detective for a short time, but she had already solved two important mysteries – one in which monkeys played a part, and this one involving a meerkat and a cow. There were bound to be others, she thought.

"You're very lucky to be such a good detective," said Pontsho.

Precious smiled modestly. She never boasted, but she was glad that she had discovered the thing that she seemed to be really good at. Most people can do at least one thing rather well, but sometimes it takes a bit of time to find out what that thing is. She had found it, and now that she had done so, she would be able to use that talent well. Many years later, she would become a famous detective – the first lady detective in Botswana – but that, of course, is a story that we shall hear about much later on.

Although they had very much enjoyed the fat cakes, there was still enough room for their normal dinner, although nobody needed very large helpings that night. Then, after the meal, it was time for them to go to bed. Pontsho went off to his shelter at the back of the house, and Precious and Teb each laid out a sleeping mat in the corner of the kitchen where Teb normally slept. Teb's mother lent Precious a spare blanket so that she could wrap herself up and keep warm for the night. Although Botswana is a hot country, the nights themselves can be cold, as they often are in deserts and other warm places.

As she lay there in the darkness, thinking of the events of the day, Precious felt happy that everything had worked out so well. The cow was safely back and in due course she would have her calf. In fact, although nobody knew it at the time, the cow was due to have twins. That was very welcome news for the family, as it meant that they would have two calves to sell rather than one. And it meant, too, that they would be able to buy shoes for Teb and Pontsho, which was a very good thing.

Teb must have been very tired, as she dropped off to sleep almost straightaway. Precious, though, remained awake a bit longer, and she was still awake when a

small furry creature crept through the
door and made his way to where she was
lying. The first thing she knew of him was
the feel of his tiny moist nose sniffing at
her cheek.

She did not say anything to Kosi, as she
did not want to wake Teb. So she simply
stroked the tiny meerkat gently and
allowed him to cuddle up to her. He was
tired too, and after a few minutes she felt
his breathing change and she knew he was

asleep. In nature, meerkats sleep together in a burrow they make underground. They lie with their tiny arms about one another – a whole family of meerkats – safe and sound in their underground house. Above them, in the moonlight, there are all sorts of dangers – owls and snakes and other enemies – but they are safe down below, huddled together for warmth.

Precious drifted off to sleep eventually. She dreamed that night of cows and meerkats and tracks in the sand. She dreamed, too, of fat cakes and happy people and of her friends and of how good it felt to have been able to help them. Because helping other people *is* a good thing, whether or not you are a detective.

And in the morning, do you know, Kosi was still there, his paws under his chin, his bright black eyes closed. But the sun came up, floating slowly up into the sky, and all three of them awoke at much the same time when the kitchen filled with light.

"Another day," said Teb, rubbing the sleep from her eyes.

"Yes," said Precious, sitting up on her sleeping mat. "Another day."

And Kosi, of course, said nothing, but as Precious looked at the tiny meerkat, she was sure that he was smiling.

AFRICA AFRICA AFRICA AFRICA AFRICA AFRICA

Botswana

Alexander McCall Smith

Precious and the Mystery of the Missing Lion

THE GIRL IN THIS PICTURE is called Precious. That was her first name, and her second name was Ramotswe, and when all this happened she was nine. Nine is a good age to be. Some people like being nine so much that they really want to stay that age forever. They usually turn ten, however, and then they find out that being ten is not all that bad either. Precious, of course, was very happy being nine.

Like many of us, Precious had a number of aunts – three in fact. One of these aunts lived in the village in Botswana where

Precious was born, while another lived on an ostrich farm almost one hundred miles away. And a third, who was probably her favourite aunt of all, lived right up at the top of the country, in a place called the Okavango Delta. That's a lovely name, isn't it? Try saying it. OKA-VANGO.

A delta, of course, is made up of small rivers spreading out from a bigger river, a little bit like a human hand and its fingers. Here's a picture of one.

Usually deltas are on the edge of the sea – this one was not. The great Okavango River flowed *backwards* – away from the sea, to spread out into smaller streams that simply sank into the sands of

a desert. And where this happened, there were wide plains of golden grass dotted with trees. On the bank of the river itself, the trees towered high. That was a bit like a proper jungle, and you had to be very careful when making your way through it. It was all very wild, and was home to just about every sort of wild animal to be found in Africa.

The aunt who lived up there was called Aunty Bee. Precious had been told her real name, but had forgotten it. Nobody ever called Aunty Bee anything but Bee. It was just the way it was.

Aunty Bee was not one of those aunts who scold you or tell you what to do. She was fun. She was also very generous and never forgot to send Precious a present on her birthday. And what presents these were! They were all made by Aunty Bee herself, from things that she could pick up in the bush around her.

One year there was a hat made entirely out of porcupine quills. As you know, porcupines are very prickly animals that have coats made of extraordinary black-and-white quills. These are sharp, and if anything tries to attack the porcupine all that he has to do is shoot out these quills. The animal attacking him then learns a very painful lesson: do not try to eat a porcupine! Indeed, some say that this is the very first lesson that a mother lion or leopard teaches her children: *do not try to eat a porcupine!* Unfortunately, some of them do not listen, and this is what happens:

The porcupine hat was made of quills that Aunty Bee had found lying around on a path. She picked these up and took them to make into a hat. This was the result.

Precious was very proud of it.

"What a beautiful hat," people remarked. "May we touch it?"

"Yes," said Precious. "But I wouldn't, if I were you!"

Another present Aunty Bee sent one year was a bracelet made of twisted elephant hair. This was very special, as people said that elephant hair was lucky.

Such bracelets were also very rare, as the elephant hair had to be plucked from the end of the elephant's tail, and it was very dangerous to do that. Elephants do not like you to pull their tails, even if all you want is to borrow a few hairs for a bracelet.

Aunty Bee bought that elephant hair from a man who was very thin. People said that an elephant had sat on him and squashed him a bit, but nobody knew whether or not that was true. But it certainly made an interesting story to tell to people who admired the bracelet.

And there were other presents, too. There was a cup made out of the seed-pod of a great baobob tree. These trees are very wide and fat: so wide that it can take twenty people holding hands to go all the way round them. That's what this picture shows. Think of that! Twenty people!

It was not just on her birthday that Precious heard from her Aunty Bee. Often a letter would arrive with news of what was happening up at the safari camp

where she worked. A safari camp is a place where people go to make expeditions into the wilderness. They go out for days on end to see wild animals and take photographs of them. They live in tents and eat out in the open and usually enjoy themselves very much indeed.

The camp that Aunty Bee worked in was called Eagle Island Camp. She was one of the cooks there, but she also earned a bit of money telling stories to the visitors. She knew all the old Botswana stories and would recite these beside the fireside at night. People loved to hear these and would clap and clap after she finished.

Aunty Bee was very busy but she always seemed to find the time to write to Precious, even if the letters were not very long – one or two lines perhaps. And it was in one of these short letters that she asked Precious whether she would like to come up to visit her.

"Dear Precious," she wrote, "I know that the school holidays are coming up soon. Would you like to come and stay with me up at the safari camp for a few days? Something very exciting is about to happen. I do hope you can come. With love, Aunty Bee."

How would you answer a letter like that? Exactly – so would I!

WHEN PRECIOUS showed this letter to her father, Obed Ramotswe, he looked doubtful.

"It's a long way away," he said. "It takes a whole day to get there – sometimes more."

"I don't mind," said Precious. "There are buses that go that way, aren't there?"

Obed scratched his head. "That costs money," he said. "And I've had a lot of bills to pay this month."

Precious tried not to show her disappointment. Her father was kind to her, and she knew that he would do anything to make her happy. If he said that there was no money for the bus fare, then she knew that this would be true.

"Perhaps I can go some other time," she said quietly. "I'll write to Aunty Bee and tell her."

Obed held up a hand. "No," he said. "Don't do that. I think I may know somebody who's going up there for four or five days. He's a cattle buyer and he has some business to do in those parts. He might be able to give you a ride up in his truck."

Precious hardly dared hope. "Do you think so?" she asked. "I wouldn't take up much room."

Her father smiled. "I'll ask him," he said. "He owes me a favour, anyway."

That evening, Precious wrote a reply to her aunt telling her that there was a chance – just a chance – she would be able

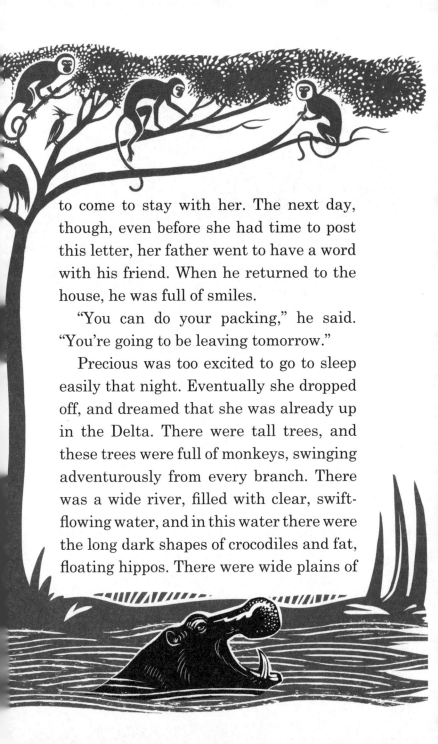

to come to stay with her. The next day, though, even before she had time to post this letter, her father went to have a word with his friend. When he returned to the house, he was full of smiles.

"You can do your packing," he said. "You're going to be leaving tomorrow."

Precious was too excited to go to sleep easily that night. Eventually she dropped off, and dreamed that she was already up in the Delta. There were tall trees, and these trees were full of monkeys, swinging adventurously from every branch. There was a wide river, filled with clear, swift-flowing water, and in this water there were the long dark shapes of crocodiles and fat, floating hippos. There were wide plains of

high grass, and in this grass, half-hidden and staring out with large yellow eyes, there were lions.

She awoke to her father's voice.

"Time to get up, my darling," he said. "The truck will be here any moment now."

She leapt out of bed and dressed quickly. Her father had made her a breakfast of thick porridge and goat's milk, and she ate this while he checked that she had everything she needed. There was a little bit of money – not much – tied up in an old handkerchief. "You can use that to buy yourself a treat," he said.

She wiped the traces of milk from her lips. "I'll buy you a present," she said.

"You don't need to do that," he said, smiling. "You may need some food on the way. Use it for something like that."

There came the sound of a horn from the road outside.

"That'll be the truck," said her father. "Off you go, now."

Obed's friend was called Mr Poletsi. He was travelling with his wife, who was called Mma Poletsi, and there were ten passengers – friends and friends of friends – who had crowded into the back of the

truck. The Poletsis sat in the front, in the cab, while everybody else made themselves as comfortable as they could in the back. There were also several chickens in a small coop, a dog tied to somebody's toe with a piece of string, and a baby goat. Precious thought it a very strange mixture, but the important thing for her was that she was on her way to see her aunt. That was all that mattered, she thought.

In spite of the fact that the truck was crowded, everybody seemed to be in a good mood and very happy to be travelling

together. Some of the others had brought
food with them, and this they shared with
their fellow passengers. Precious knew
that this was very important. She had
been taught to share, as people are taught
in Africa, and if she had had any food with
her she would have shared it too.

At the beginning of the journey, it was
cool enough sitting in the back of the truck,
but as the day wore on it became hotter
and hotter. Now, with the midday sun
directly above them in the sky, it became
very uncomfortable for the passengers

and Precious would have given anything to be sitting in the comfort of the cab with the Poletsis, but she knew that this was impossible.

They stopped at a small store along the side of the road and they were able to have a long drink of water before continuing. This helped, but after half an hour or so she began to feel thirsty again.

"I hope we arrive soon," she said to the woman sitting beside her.

The woman laughed. "Oh, we won't arrive soon," she said. "We've still got hundreds of miles to go."

"When will we arrive?" asked Precious.

"Midnight, I think," said the woman. "Not before."

The road was straight and narrow, with very little traffic on it. For mile after mile it ran across great empty plains that stretched out on either side as far as the eye could see. And it was while they were crossing one of these plains that the

truck's engine suddenly coughed and died. One moment it was working and the next moment there was silence as the truck drew slowly to a halt.

They all got out. Mr Poletsi opened the front of the truck and looked at the engine. He soon enough found the problem – a broken fan-belt. "This is very bad," he said. "We'll have to wait until somebody comes past. Then I can ask them to take me to the nearest town. I'll find a new fan-belt and come back with it."

"But that could take hours," said one of the passengers. "We may be here the whole night."

"I see no other way," said Mr Poletsi. And then he added: "Unless anybody else has got any bright ideas?"

Precious looked at the fan-belt. It had been a complete circle, a bit like a massive elastic band – now it was just a single strip of rather sad-looking rubber.

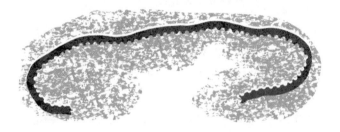

She looked down. She was wearing the belt that her father had bought her a few weeks before. She was very proud of it, but this was clearly an emergency.

"Has anybody got some string?" she asked.

The woman who had been sitting beside her replied that she had some and passed it to her.

Precious took off her belt. Carefully threading the string through one of the holes in the belt, she made it into a strong circle, exactly the size of the broken fan-belt.

Mr Poletsi was watching her. "You clever girl," he exclaimed. "I can see what you're doing."

The makeshift fan-belt fitted perfectly. Mr Poletsi then closed the engine compartment and went back to his place in the cab. There was an anxious moment as everybody waited to see whether the truck would start. But it did, and it ran perfectly sweetly with the repair that Precious had made.

"I think you should come and sit with us in the cabin," said Mma Poletsi. "As a reward for what you've done."

Everybody agreed that this was well-deserved, and so Precious made the rest of the journey in comfort, snuggling up against Mma Poletsi in the cab while the sun dropped down below the horizon. She felt proud and happy, and of course excited. Very soon she would be seeing Aunty Bee and finding out what the exciting thing was that her aunt had talked about.

THEY ARRIVED AT EAGLE ISLAND Camp by
night. It was very different from home,
where the lights of houses and of cars
meant that it was never really dark; here
in the bush there was complete darkness,
with only one or two tiny pin-pricks of
light showing from a camp-fire or a hut.
Precious was sleepy, and Aunty Bee said
that she should go straight to bed.

"You'll see where you are when you wake
up in the morning," she said. "There'll be
plenty of time to explore then."

Her aunt had laid out a mattress on the
floor in her own room, and Precious found
this very comfortable. She closed her eyes

and in less than a minute she was fast asleep, not waking up until the first rays of the sun came through the window the next day.

She looked about her, half-forgetting where she was. But then she remembered, and got up to dress herself as quickly as she could. There were sounds coming from the kitchen next door, which meant that Aunty Bee was already preparing breakfast.

She greeted her aunt and sat down at the table. Through the open door of the kitchen she could see that Aunty Bee's house was in the middle of a circle of small buildings that housed the people who worked in the safari camp. Not far away, at the end of a path that ran through a clump of very high trees, was the camp itself. This was made up of thatched huts on the edge of a river, all joined to one another by a raised wooden walkway. It looked like a very exciting place to stay.

Aunty Bee served her a bowl of porridge

and a thick slice of bread spread with jam she had made herself. While Precious was eating this, she listened to the story her aunt had to tell.

"There is something very special happening," Aunty Bee began. "We have some film-makers arriving today. Everybody is very excited."

Precious felt excited too, and asked what sort of film they were making.

"It's about a man who gets lost in the jungle," said Aunty Bee. "I don't know the full story, but they have lots of people coming with cameras and lights and all the other things they need to make a film. We're going to be very busy."

Aunty Bee would have more cooking to do, she said, once all the film people arrived. "You'll have to entertain yourself," she said to Precious. "But please be careful. Don't wander away from the camp by yourself – there are plenty of wild animals around here."

Precious promised that she would

be very careful. "I won't go near any elephants," she said. "And I'll keep well away from lions too!"

After they had finished their breakfast, Aunty Bee went off to work, promising to return just before lunchtime to check that everything was all right. There were other children nearby, she said, and she was sure that Precious would meet them.

Precious said goodbye to her aunt and waved to her as she made her way along the path to the main camp. Then she did a bit of tidying-up to help Aunty Bee, before she went outside to explore. She hoped that she would see some of the other children, but there seemed to be none around. So she decided to go down to the edge of the river, which was not very far away from the staff houses.

That was her first mistake – and it was a bad one. Nobody had warned her about hippos – perhaps they had meant to do so and had forgotten, or perhaps they just thought that she knew what dangerous and

bad-tempered creatures they could be.

Certainly the hippo that Precious came across was not in a good temper. As she came down to the edge of the river, the hippo suddenly rose from the water, fixed her with an angry stare, and opened his great mouth to issue a resounding grunt. It was a very frightening noise, and it sounded something like this:

For a moment Precious stood quite still, too petrified to move. Then, turning on her heels, she ran back up the path as fast as her legs would carry her. Which was quite fast, of course, as most people run rather quickly when they meet an angry hippo. And as she ran round a corner, she bumped straight into a boy of about her age who was standing in the path wondering what the noise was all about.

"There's a hippo down there!" shouted Precious, struggling to recover her breath.

The boy, whose name was Khumo (you say it KOO-MO), did not seem surprised.

"Oh, that's just Harry," he said. "He's always down there. He's a very lazy hippo and has never chased anybody."

Precious was relieved, but she had still had a dreadful fright. "He looked very fierce," she said.

Khumo smiled. "Well, let's leave him in peace. Why don't you come with me now and see what's happening in the camp. It's something very exciting. There's a lion."

Precious was not sure that she wanted

to meet a lion so soon after her encounter with the hippo, but Khumo seemed to know what he was doing. So she followed him back along the track, wondering all the while what would await them when they reached the camp.

A
S THEY MADE THEIR WAY to the main camp, Khumo told Precious about the lion.

"Most of the lions around here are wild ones," he said. "This one, though, is not from here. He came with the film-makers. He's an actor lion."

Precious looked puzzled and asked her new friend to explain.

"They brought him with them," he said. "He's tame. They're going to use him in the film they're making."

Precious nodded; now she understood. She had heard about dogs that had been

trained to act in films – to fetch things and so on – but she had never heard of a lion doing this.

"Are you sure he's completely tame?" she asked nervously. They were now getting close to the camp and she could see people milling around. She could also see a large cage in which something – and it must have been the actor lion – was moving.

"Everybody says he is," Khumo replied. "Anyway, we'll soon find out. It looks as if they're going to let him out of his cage."

They had now reached the camp and were standing with some of the film people near the lion's cage. There was a tall man wearing a large brown hat who seemed to be in charge of the lion.

"Let him out now, Tom," said somebody to this man, who then stepped forward and opened the door of the cage.

Precious gave a shiver as the great lion came out into the sunlight. Nobody else, though, seemed to be worried, and Tom, the man with the large hat, went forward

to pat the lion on the head.

"You see?" said Khumo. "He's tame. You couldn't do that to a lion who wasn't tame, could you?"

Precious had to agree that you could not.

The children watched as the film crew set about their work. The scene they were filming had two actors walking across a piece of ground and seeing the lion, called Teddy by everyone, sitting under a tree.

Tom took Teddy to the tree and told him
to sit under it.

"Sit, Teddy," he said. And Teddy, like a
well-trained dog, sat down obediently.

There were cameras mounted on trolleys
and there was a lot of shouting and rushing
about. Nobody seemed to mind Precious
and Khumo watching, and at one point
somebody even asked them to hold onto a
cable while it was being wound up. This
made them feel very important – as if they

were members of the film crew itself. And later on, when everybody took a break, the two children were handed large mugs of sweet tea and the fattest fat cake they had ever seen. A fat cake is a special treat in Botswana. This is what it looks like.

It tastes just like a doughnut, but more delicious, if that is possible.

Precious and Khumo ate their fat cakes and were licking the sugar off their fingers when Tom came over to ask them to help.

"We want to film Teddy standing up suddenly and looking at something in the grass," he said. "Would you mind hiding in the grass, and then, when I give you the signal, making some sort of sound to attract his attention. Maybe a sort of clucking sound, as if you're a guinea fowl.

Lions like guinea fowl, you know, and that will be bound to interest him."

They felt very important to have a job to do, and they both went off to hide in the grass as Tom had asked them. As they lay there, Precious suddenly had a worrying thought.

"What if he thinks we really are guinea fowl?" she whispered to Khumo.

"He won't," said Khumo. "He's a very clever lion."

"I hope so," said Precious. "Because if he really thought we were guinea fowl, then he might pounce on us."

They waited quietly, the only sound being that of their beating hearts. Precious thought that her heart was beating rather loudly – and so did Khumo. That's the trouble about being frightened – you may be as quiet as you can manage, but your heart doesn't seem to take much notice.

"Right," called Tom. "Please attract Teddy's attention now."

Precious and Khumo both started to make the noise that a guinea fowl makes. It sounded a bit like the noise a hen makes, only it was a bit more … well, spotted. This is what it sounded like.

At first Teddy did nothing.

"Perhaps he's feeling a bit sleepy," whispered Khumo. "I think we should be a bit louder."

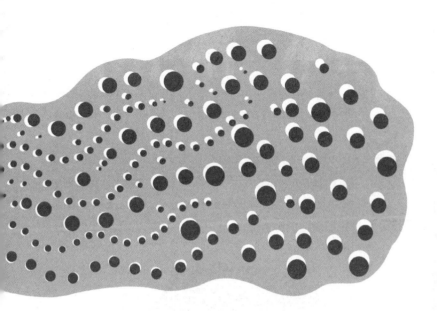

They raised the volume of the noise and, sure enough, Teddy's ears started to prick up. Then he sat up and looked with interest in their direction. After that, things happened very quickly – so quickly, in fact, that neither Precious nor Khumo had much time to react.

With one great bound, Teddy reached the edge of the clump of tall grass in which the two children were hiding. Then, with another not quite so long bound, he was upon them.

Precious closed her eyes. If you were

going to be eaten by a lion, then she thought it was probably best not to see what was happening. But then she felt a rather rough, wet tongue licking at her face, moving on to her neck, finally getting to her knees. It was a bit like being tickled, and she could not stop herself from laughing.

Teddy had pounced on them not to eat them or to scratch them, but to play. Now he was lying on the ground, his feet up in the air, inviting them to scratch his stomach. It was very funny.

Tom was very pleased with what his cameras had seen, and they all went back to the camp for tea and more fat cakes.

"You did very well," Tom said to Precious and Khumo. "Please stay with us and help us for the rest of the day."

"Certainly," said Precious.

And Khumo, without any hesitation, said the same thing.

CHAPTER
FIVE

I T PROVED TO BE AN EXCITING DAY. And
the day after that was exciting too,
as there was filming to be done deep
in the forest. That meant a long ride in a
truck – with Teddy – along a very bumpy
and overgrown track.

Tom was very pleased with the work
that Precious and Khumo did, and he made
sure that at the end of the day they were
rewarded with an envelope full of money.
That suited them very well, as they were
both saving for things, and the money
would be very helpful for that.

But then, at the end of the second day,
just after they had returned to the camp

and Precious was back in Aunty Bee's house, they heard the sound of people shouting and calling. Something had clearly happened, and when Precious and her aunt went outside, they found out what it was.

"Teddy's disappeared!" shouted one of the film men. "We don't know where he is."

Precious joined the throng of people from the camp who started looking for the missing lion. They searched under the trucks and vans; they searched in the sheds where they kept supplies; they even looked under the beds in some of the camp huts just in case he had decided to find a

hiding place there. But there was no sign
of him – Teddy, it seemed, had vanished
into thin air.

Darkness came down like a curtain.
Now it was too late to search any more,
and they all had to go to bed hoping that
in the morning he would come out from
wherever he was hiding in time for that
day's filming.

"He'll turn up," said Aunty Bee. "Or at
least I hope he'll turn up."

The next morning, when the sun rose
up over the tops of the trees like a great
red ball, Precious went outside to look for
Teddy. She studied the ground, as her

father had taught her to do, for any sign that a lion had walked that way, but there was nothing. She saw the footprints of a small family of warthogs,

but nothing that looked like the large pug-marks that a lion leaves behind.

After breakfast, when she went down to the camp with Khumo, they saw Tom sitting unhappily beneath a tree, his head sunk in his hands.

"I don't know what to do," he said. "Without Teddy, we'll have to change the whole story of our film."

Precious felt very sorry for the director. It was not easy to make a film, and when one of the stars decides to disappear it must make it even more difficult.

"I think we should try to help him," she said to Khumo. "I think we should go and look for him."

Khumo was uncertain. "But will they let us?" he asked.

"I can ask Aunty Bee," said Precious.

She went to her aunt and explained what she and Khumo wanted to do. "If we are very, very, very careful," she said, "will you let us go off and look for the missing lion?"

Aunty Bee looked doubtful. "There are rather a lot of elephants about," she said. "And hippos too. Not to mention all those snakes ..."

"We won't go near any of them," said Precious. "I promise."

Aunty Bee had a canoe. She did not use it very much, but it still floated and as far as she knew there were no holes in it, which was a good thing, as holes in any sort of boat are not a very good idea.

"I suppose you can take my canoe," she said after a while. "But keep well away from hippos."

"We will," said Precious, as she ran off to tell Khumo the good news.

They set off about an hour later. Precious had packed some sandwiches – enough for both of them – and she also brought a spare hat, and a compass to use in case they got lost. Khumo brought a bag of toffees, a small box of sticking plasters, a

box of matches, and two bottles of water.
They had everything they needed.

The canoe was an old-fashioned one,
made of wood and propelled through the
water with two stout paddles. It was a
little bit wobbly, but canoes often are and
you quickly get used to them. Soon they
were slipping through the water of the
great river, and after half an hour they
were well into the wild forests and plains
that surrounded the camp.

They looked about them very carefully as they made their way. There was plenty to see on the banks of the river. There were great trees from which vines hung down like swinging ropes. There were slippery patches of mud used by crocodiles

to launch themselves into the water. There were places where herds of zebra and antelopes came nervously down to the edge of the river to drink, watching all the time for lions that might creep up behind them, or crocodiles that might lurk in the

water in front of them. It was dangerous being a zebra or antelope as there were plenty of other creatures round about who might imagine that you were just right for their breakfast, lunch or even their dinner.

After a few hours of paddling, they stopped on a small island in the middle of the river. Beaching the canoe, they found some comfortable grass on which to have their picnic of the sandwiches that Precious

had prepared. They were very hungry, as paddling a canoe takes a lot of energy and breakfast had been some time ago.

They had just finished their last sandwich when Precious noticed a movement on the riverbank opposite their island.

"What was that?" she asked Khumo, shading her eyes from the bright glare of the sun. "I think I saw something over there."

Khumo rose to his feet – slowly, so

as not to disturb whatever it was that Precious had seen. "I can't see anything," he said. But then, quite suddenly, he did see something, and it made him take in his breath with a gasp.

"Lions," he whispered. "A whole pride of them."

"Sit down," whispered Precious. "We don't want them to see us."

They remained quite still as the pride of lions made its way down to the water to drink. There were six of them altogether,

and it did not take long for Precious and Khumo to identify which one was Teddy.

"That's him," whispered Khumo, pointing to a lion standing on the edge of the group.

Precious saw that it was Teddy. He seemed to be quite happy with his new friends, and they watched them all until, at a signal from the biggest lion, who was also the leader – a roar – they turned round and made their way back into the bush.

Once the lions had gone, Precious and

Khumo pushed their canoe back into the water, climbed into it, and paddled back down the river. They did not take a break on the way back, as they wanted to get to Tom as soon as possible to give him the good news that they had found his missing lion.

TOM WAS VERY PLEASED.

"Do you remember exactly where you saw the lions?" he asked. "Will you be able to take us to them?"

Khumo looked a bit doubtful. "I think so," he began. "It was where the river went a bit like this ..." He made a movement of his hands. "And then it went a bit like this ..." He made another movement to show a change of direction.

Tom looked worried. Rivers were always going like this, and then this, and he was not sure whether Khumo's directions would be good enough. But he did not know, of course, that Precious was the girl who was destined to become Botswana's most famous detective, and that she had stored away in her memory every detail of the trip down the river.

"Excuse me," she said. "I know exactly where the spot is. It is after the river turns to the left just before you reach a very old tree that has half fallen into the water. There are some sand banks in the middle of the river that are about as deep as the top of my knees, and then there is an island that has a bush at one end, a clump of rocks at the other, and an ant-hill in the middle. The lions came down to drink on the shore right on the other side. So they'll

be somewhere near there."

Tom looked impressed. "You are a very observant girl," he said. "I'm sure that will help us to find the place."

Precious smiled modestly. She was not at all boastful, and she wanted to make sure that Khumo would get some of any praise that was being given. "Khumo helped a lot," she said.

Tom thanked Khumo too, and it was agreed that once everybody was ready, they would set off once again to see if they could find Teddy. Precious was not sure how they would manage to get him back – particularly if he was having a good time with his new lion friends – but Tom seemed to think this would not be too hard.

"He's a very tame lion," he said. "I'm sure that once he finds that he has to hunt for his food and not have it delivered to him in a big dish, he will be less keen to stay out in the wild."

There was enough time before they left for Precious to go and tell her aunt all about their adventure. Aunty Bee was relieved that they had got home without getting into any trouble, and was very proud of the fact that they had managed to find Teddy. She was perfectly happy for Precious to go out again, this time with Tom and the other people from the film crew.

"They'll look after you,' she said. And

then she stopped and thought. "Or maybe *you* will be the one to look after *them*."

Precious smiled. "We'll see," she said.

Aunty Bee looked at her fondly. "You know something?" she said. "Your father said that he thought you had the makings of a great detective. And I think he might be right."

They took a much bigger boat this time – large enough for ten people to sit in it quite comfortably and not get at all wet. This boat had an engine, and it made a throaty roar as they set off from the camp. Precious looked back and waved to her aunt, and Khumo waved too, continuing to do so until they rounded a bend in the river and lost sight of the camp.

It did not take them long to make the trip. There were quite a few islands, but Tom was able to identify the right one from the description that Precious had given. Now they were in sight of the place on the shore where the lions had been, and were able to steer their boat gently in to the muddy bank.

They got their feet a bit wet as they went ashore, but the water was warm and that did not matter.

"We must be very quiet now," said Tom, putting a finger to his lips. "Lions have very good hearing and we don't want them to take fright and run away."

Once everybody was on dry land and the boat had been firmly tied to a tree trunk at the edge of the water, the whole party began to walk very slowly and carefully through the thick grass and scrub bush. Tom led the way, and then came one of

his men, and behind them were Precious and Khumo. The other men who had come with them brought up the rear, looking anxiously around them from time to time.

"You have to be very careful when looking for lions," Tom whispered. "Sometimes when you are looking for a lion, the lion creeps round behind you and then, before you know what's happened, you're being stalked by the lion rather than the other way round."

Precious gave a shiver when she heard this. She did not like the thought of a lion creeping up behind her.

"Don't worry," said Khumo. "Tom will be very careful."

"I hope so," said Precious.

They walked for about an hour. "No sign of anything yet," said Tom. "Have you seen any tracks?"

Precious shook her head. "Only old ones," she said. 'I think lions must have been here once, but I think it was quite a few days ago – maybe even weeks."

She had just finished saying this when she noticed something. It was not something that most people would notice, but you have to remember that she was a detective-in-training and so she saw things that other people walked right past.

"Wait," she said, her voice low. "Look at this."

The whole line of people came to a stop.

"What have you found?" asked Tom.

Precious pointed to a bush at the side of the rough track they were following. One of the branches had been bent back so that it had snapped. There was still fresh sap where the break had happened.

"Something passed by this way not all that long ago," she said. "Some big animal."

"But it could have been anything," said Tom. "A zebra. A buffalo. Anything."

Precious was now down on her hands and knees, examining the ground. "No," she said. "It was a lion. Several lions, in fact. Look at these."

Tom and Khumo, along with the other men who were with them, now bent down to look at the ground where Precious was pointing.

Khumo, whose father was a game scout

who had taught him how to track wild animals, saw what his friend meant. "Precious is right," he said. "Lions went this way – and only a few minutes ago."

At the news that the lions had been there only a few minutes earlier, Tom and his men looked a bit anxious.

"I hope they're not too close," said one of the men, giving a little shiver as he spoke.

"We'll soon find out," said Precious. "Let's follow their tracks – keeping a careful look-out, of course."

"A *very* careful look-out," said Tom.

THEY WENT FORWARD SLOWLY, looking down at the ground very carefully before they put down their feet. This was so that they should not step on a twig that might snap and give them away to any creature that was listening. And lions do listen for anything that is coming their way – they are also very watchful animals, even if they are big and fierce and have large teeth that are very good at biting ... Precious did not like to think of that, and neither, I imagine, do you.

It was Precious who spotted them first. At first she thought it was just one of those tricks that your eyes can play. She

thought it might just be a branch swaying
in the breeze, or the shadow of a tiny cloud
moving across the ground. But then she
realised that it was neither of these, and
that what she was looking at was a lion.

Once she knew that, then in an instant
she saw all the rest. She saw that what
looked like a pile of brown leaves on the
ground was actually a young lion lying
with his head on his front paws. And then
what looked like a bendy branch in front of
a bush was in fact a large lioness that was

standing quite still looking up at the sky. Altogether she saw six lions, and they were not far away, really probably not much further than you or I could throw a small stone.

She reached out to tap Khumo on the shoulder. He turned round, looked where she was pointing, and then he let out a very low whistle to alert Tom.

"Over there," whispered Khumo. "Look!"

Precious and Khumo both knew that

they were safe as long as they made no sudden movements or sounds. This was because the wind was blowing from the direction of the lions. Had it been blowing the other way, then the lions would have smelled them very easily. Lions have a good sense of smell, and can tell when people or other animals are nearby just by lifting their great lion noses into the air and sniffing at the breeze.

Tom studied the lions and the way they were lying around resting. After a few moments, he whispered to Precious and Khumo, telling them what his plan was.

"Teddy is right on the edge of the pride," he said. "See him over there?"

They looked. Sure enough, Teddy was some distance away from the others, under the shade provided by a tree. He seemed to be having his afternoon nap.

"I'm going to creep up towards him," Tom went on. "There's quite a bit of cover, and that means that they won't see me.

Once I reach him, he'll remember me, of course, and will come back here with me. He always obeys me, especially if I offer him one of his lion treats."

He showed them a large biscuit – rather like a dog biscuit – that he was holding in his right hand.

"Isn't that a bit dangerous?" asked Precious. "What if the other lions see you? What then?"

"They won't see me," said Tom. "I will be very careful."

Precious glanced at Khumo, who shrugged. It seemed as if he thought that if this was what Tom wanted to do, then he could not do anything to stop him. After all, Tom was an adult, and it is often rather difficult for children to stop adults from doing things once they have made up their minds to do it.

Dropping to his hands and knees, Tom began to crawl through the undergrowth. He moved very slowly, and he was well-covered by the grass and bushes, so Precious stopped worrying quite so much that he would be seen. Perhaps Tom really knew what he was doing after all, she thought.

But then something dreadful happened. It was so dreadful that Precious almost gave a shriek when she discovered it. Fortunately she did not, because that would have made matters a whole lot worse.

What happened was that she suddenly saw that at the other edge of the clearing another lion had woken up and was

showing his face. That face was Teddy's – she was absolutely sure of it. The lion that Tommy was now approaching looked like Teddy, but that was all. He was definitely not the tame actor lion, but was a wild lion that would not be very interested in being offered a lion treat by a man on his hands and knees. For such a lion, it would not be the biscuit, but the man himself who would seem like a tasty lion afternoon snack.

Precious had to act quickly. She could not call out to Tom, as that would disturb all the other lions, making them immediately come bounding towards them. So she would have to do something quite different – which is what she now did.

First she picked up a stone. Then, half rising, she made her best imitation of a guinea fowl. She sounded something like this.

Then, with every ounce of strength she had, she threw the stone up into the air to the other side of the clearing – well away from where Tom was crawling through the grass.

At the sound of the guinea fowl, all the lions in the pride rose to their feet and looked about them with interest. Then, when the stone landed in a thick clump of bush well away from the humans, the lions all bounded off to investigate. Lions, as you know, cannot resist guinea fowl and the thought that there might be a plump guinea fowl so close to them was just too much of a temptation.

Tom saw what was happening. The
moment the lion towards which he was
crawling rose to his feet, he knew that he
had made a terrible mistake. He froze, not
moving while the great lion rushed past
him. Then, when the danger was over and
the lions were all sniffing about in the
bush for a guinea fowl that was not there,
Tom crawled back to join the others as

fast as his knees would carry him.

"Thank you," he whispered to Precious as they made their way hurriedly back down the track towards the boat. "You saved my life, you know."

He thanked her again when they reached the boat, and he repeated his thanks when they arrived back at the camp. That was exactly what he should have done. If somebody saves your life, then you should thank him or her at least three times. And if you are particularly grateful, you can say thank you a fourth time, which is what he did that night over dinner round the camp fire. Precious had been invited and sat there modestly while Tom told the story. Then everybody clapped and cheered, which made Precious feel a bit embarrassed. She was a modest girl, you see, and she had simply done what she had to do.

THE NEXT DAY there was a meeting of Tom and all the film crew. Precious and Aunty Bee were invited, as was Khumo.

"We are going to have to try to get Teddy back again," said Tom. "This time we are going to take a famous lion catcher with us. He will be arriving with his net just before lunch time."

Precious looked at the ground. She did not like the thought of Teddy being caught in a net. That would have been a very frightening experience for any lion, particularly for a gentle lion like Teddy.

Tom noticed that Precious looked upset.

"Is there anything wrong with my plan?" he asked.

Precious bit her lip. She was not sure how to say what she wanted to say, but then Aunty Bee said something that helped make up her mind. "It's always better to speak the things that are in your heart," she whispered. "Never be too shy to do that."

Precious knew that her aunt was right. And her father had told her the same thing too. "Don't bite your tongue and say nothing when you feel that you have to speak. People respect a person who says what she thinks."

Now she looked up. "I don't think you should catch him," she said. "I think that he's happy being free."

This was greeted with silence.

"But he's an actor," said Tom at last. "His place is with us – in the films. He has a job to do!"

"His place is with other lions," said Precious. "That is where he will be happiest. Lions like to be with other lions – that is well known."

Tom opened his mouth to say something else, but then he closed it.

"I think we should leave him," Precious went on. "Those other lions will teach him how to hunt and to live in the wild again. He will learn how to sleep under the stars. He will learn how to wash his paws in rivers. He will learn how to roll about in a dust bath and jump up in the air to catch a guinea fowl as it flies from the grass. He

will learn a lot of things that lions need to know." She paused. "That *real* lions need to know."

She stopped, because everybody was looking at her.

"Is that all?" Tom finally asked.

"Yes," she said. "I hope you don't think me rude, but that is what I really feel."

Tom waited a moment before replying.

"I think you're right," he said. "You've made me see it from Teddy's point of view – from the lion's point of view. I've never done that before – I've always thought of myself. Now I know I'm wrong."

"I agree," said Tom's assistant.

"And I agree too," said the head cameraman. "We've already got plenty of

shots of lions that we can use."

Precious thought of something else. "But there's one other thing," she said. "I think we should go back there to say goodbye. We can do that from the boat – it won't be dangerous if we do it that way."

They all agreed, and so a few hours later they set off again, this time taking Aunty Bee with them. She had time to make some especially delicious sandwiches, that they ate as the boat drifted down the river towards the place where the lions liked to drink from the edge of the water.

The lions were there. This time it was Khumo who saw them first, and he excitedly pointed them out to everybody else on the boat. Teddy was with them – there was no mistaking him – and when

they approached in their boat, keeping a safe distance away, he came down to the edge of the water and sniffed at the air.

For a few moments Precious wondered whether he was going to try to swim out to see them. He looked at them, and he moved his head up and down a bit as if he were greeting them. Then he let out a little roar. It was not an unfriendly roar; it was more of a *hello, how are you?* roar rather than a *stay away from me!* roar.

Tom raised a hand to wave to Teddy. The lion and the man looked at each other

for quite a few minutes, as if they were both remembering all the time they had spent together. Then, rather sadly, in the way in which you would leave a good friend, Teddy turned round and began to walk back to the new life he had found for himself.

That was the last night that Precious was to spend with her aunt. The following day, she was to go back home with the people who had brought her up in their truck. She was sad to be leaving Aunty Bee, but she had plenty of friends back home to whom she was looking forward to telling the story of her adventures. Khumo was sorry to see her go, but he promised to write to her and said that he hoped one day he would see her again. He knew that she was already a detective and that she would become an even better detective as the years went by.

"Perhaps you'll teach me how to be your assistant," he said. "Only if you've got the time, of course."

"Perhaps," said Precious.

That night, asleep on the floor of her aunt's room, with the sounds of the African night coming in through the window, she dreamed that she was out in the bush. In this dream she was walking along a path when she suddenly came upon a lion, and this was a lion called Teddy. And he smiled at her, in a curious, lion-like way before he ambled off back into the grass. It was not long grass, and she could see him quite

well in the dream as he bounded off into the distance.

"Goodbye!" she whispered under her breath.

And he half-turned his head, and looked back at her, and said something that she did not quite catch. She did not know what it was, but she did know that it was something happy.

This is for
Douglas Richard Mant

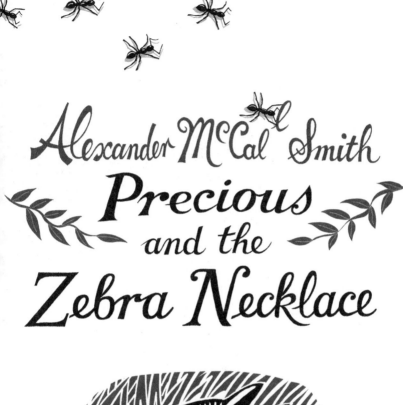

Alexander McCall Smith

Precious
and the
Zebra Necklace

AFRICA

Botswana

THIS IS THE STORY of a girl who was a private detective. Now, you may ask, what is a private detective? Well, a private detective is a person who solves mysteries for other people. So if you or I have something we really want to find out about – maybe a secret of some sort – then we may well ask a private detective to help. That's what they do. Private detectives are very good at finding out things. They look for clues. They ask all sorts of questions. They know just who did what, and when they did it.

This is a picture of a typical private detective, but here is a picture of a rather special private detective. Can you spot the difference? Well done! (And that shows that you might be a bit of a private detective yourself!) One is a woman, and the other is ... a girl.

Precious started to be a private detective when she was only nine, which is how old she was when all this happened. She was just an ordinary girl, who went to school like everybody else, and who had to remember to do her homework and so on. But in her spare time she solved mysteries, and sorted out problems for other people. She enjoyed doing this, as she was good at it, you see, and if you are good at something, then doing it is always fun.

"I like solving mysteries," Precious said to her friends. "And the more mysterious they are, the better!"

This mystery was one of those very mysterious ones, and it all started, as many such mysteries do, in an ordinary way. This is what happened.

Precious lived in Botswana, a country in Africa, and her school was at the top of a hill. Every morning the children lined up outside the classroom before going in for the start of their lessons. To help the teachers count the pupils, everyone in the line called out a number in turn, starting with number 1 and ending with ... Well, they usually ended with number 30, but on this particular morning the last number to be called out was 31. There was a new member of the class, a girl, and her name was Nancy.

"This is your new friend Nancy," announced the teacher once the children had streamed into the classroom. "And now we must find somewhere for her to sit."

Her gaze fell on Precious and the teacher's mind was made up. Precious was a kind girl, and the teacher knew that she would be helpful to somebody who was just starting at a new school.

"Sit over there," she said to Nancy. "You'll look after her, won't you, Precious?"

Precious nodded. She liked the look of the new girl, who had a very friendly smile on her face. Here is a picture of it.

A person who has a smile like that, thought Precious, *is bound to be exactly the sort of person you would want as a friend.* And that is just what happened. After no more than ten minutes, Precious and Nancy were firm friends. After half an hour, it was as if they had known one another all their lives.

That afternoon, when Precious went home after school, she told her aunt about Nancy, and about how she and Nancy had got on so well. This aunt was now living with Precious and her father, as Precious's own mother was no longer alive, and they needed somebody to run the house when Precious's father was away working with his cattle. The aunt was a cheerful woman who never seemed to be in a bad mood and was widely known as one of the best cooks in that part of Botswana.

She was also quite good at fixing cars, and at one time or another she had fixed the cars of many of their neighbours. She knew everything – not just how brakes and gearboxes worked, but also about people. That was because everybody was happy to talk to her. There are some people like that, as you know: people like to talk to them *because they listen*. This aunt was a very good listener.

Here is a picture of the aunt making a cake ... and here is a picture of her fixing a car. And here is a picture of Precious telling her aunt about the new girl at school, and the aunt is about to turn round and ask, "What did you say her name was, Precious?"

And Precious replied, "She's called

Nancy. And she lives over near the water tower. She pointed the house out to me."

Her aunt nodded. "I know those people," she said. "They have just come here. I forget where they lived before this, but I think it was far away. That little girl has no mother – a bit like you."

"Her mother died?" asked Precious.

The aunt shrugged. "I don't know what happened. But those people have looked after her since she was very small. They are very kind."

That was all that she said about Nancy, and the aunt then went on to talk about a special cake that she was planning to bake. She had been given a large packet of raisins, and raisins were just right for the sort of cake she wanted to make.

Precious agreed. She liked all sorts of cake, but her aunt's cakes were far and away the best she had tasted. Here is a picture of one of them. If you scratch the picture ever so gently with one of your fingernails, you may just be able to get the smell of that cake. The smell is not coming from the page, of course – it's coming from inside your head. Can you smell it? I can – and it smells delicious.

SCRATCH SCRATCH!

Precious thought about Nancy before she dropped off to sleep that night. It is always nice to have a new friend, as having a new friend can give you a warm feeling inside — a feeling made up of excitement and interest and guesses. And yet, when she thought about Nancy, Precious also felt a little bit worried. She thought there was

something about Nancy that she was yet
to find out. It was as if her new friend had
some mystery in her life – and Precious had
no idea what that mystery might be.

Well, she thought as she drifted off to
sleep, *I'm sure I will soon find out*. And she
did – the very next day.

CHAPTER
Two

I T ALL HAPPENED because of a burst pipe. The children were sitting in their classroom the next morning, working hard on a task their teacher had set them. This was to write a letter – in very neat handwriting – to an imaginary person or a person who was well known. The teacher had shown them how to do it, writing a sample letter on the board in her very beautiful handwriting.

"You start the letter, *Dear*, and then you put in the person's name after that," explained the teacher. "Then you go on to say what you have to say – remembering

to be polite, of course – and then you sign
it off with *Yours truly*, and you put your
name after that."

A boy in the front row raised his hand.
"Why do you say *truly*?" he asked.

"It is to show them that you have not
been telling any lies," said the teacher.

"You're saying that it's all true. Any other questions?"

Nobody said anything, as they were keen to get on with practising their own letters. You did not have to know the person you were writing to, said the teacher, as this was really just a practice and the letters would not be sent.

Precious decided that she would write to the President of Botswana, which was the country in Africa where she lived.

"Dear Mr President," she began. And then she stopped to think very hard. What would she want to say to the President of Botswana if she ever had the chance to speak to him? What would any of us say if we were given the chance to speak to somebody as important as that?

She wrote the next sentence. "I would like to ask you about any plans that you have to stop people throwing litter on the ground. Please could you tell me about them. Yours truly, Precious Ramotswe."

She looked at what Nancy was writing. Her friend's letter was to the manager of the television station. Nancy was offering to read the news for them. "You won't have to pay me," she wrote, "as I will do it for nothing. My reading is quite good, and you can even ask my teacher about that if you want to check up."

Precious began to imagine what it would be like to turn on a television set and see one of your friends there. It would be very strange, she decided, although she imagined that you would get used to it after a while.

It was while she was thinking this that the water pipe just outside the classroom burst. It was an important pipe, as it provided the whole school with water, and it was also a large one. This meant that once water started spraying out of the pipe, it soon covered the ground beneath it and then began to flow into the classrooms.

The school handyman did his best to fix the pipe, but the task was beyond him. By now the level of water in the classrooms made it necessary for everybody to raise their feet off the ground, and this was becoming tiring. From her office at the end of the corridor, the principal made her mind up.

"Everybody should go home," she announced. "School is closed for the day."

Everybody was very excited and pleased. "No more school for the rest of the day!" exclaimed Precious, who liked school but also liked the idea of an unexpected holiday.

"Let's go to my house," said Nancy. "It's not far away."

Precious thought this was a very good idea, and soon the two friends were on their way to the house near the water tower.

"What can we do at your place?" asked Precious, as they left the school gate behind them.

Nancy thought for a moment before she replied. "There's something I want to show you," she said.

"What is it?" asked Precious.

Nancy gave her a special sort of smile –
the sort of smile that people give you when
they don't want to say too much just yet.
"You'll soon find out," she said.

"Give me a clue," pressed Precious. "Just
a small clue, and then let me guess."

"Zebra," said Nancy.

Precious hardly knew what to say. She
knew that people had unusual pets, but she
had never heard of anybody who had a zebra.

"You've got a zebra!" she exclaimed.

Nancy laughed. "You'll find out," she said.

Precious spent the rest of the journey wondering how you would look after a pet zebra. What would you feed it on? Was there special striped food for zebras, or did they just eat grass like horses did? And

did zebras bite – as ponies and donkeys sometimes did – or did being stripy make them gentler? And how would you find your zebra if it ran away and hid in the bush, where there were lots of striped shadows? Would you even be able to see him there?

When they arrived at the house, Precious was introduced to the people who looked

after Nancy. She called them Aunt and Uncle, and they seemed to Precious to be kind and generous people. *You can always tell when somebody is kind*, she thought: *you look into their eyes and you can see it straight away.*

"Tell me all about yourself," said the aunt. "That is, if you don't mind. You don't have to if you don't want to."

Precious smiled; she did not mind at all. And so she told the aunt and the uncle about how she lived with her father. She told them about her own aunts and about the cattle they kept. She told them about the school on the hill and about the fun they all had there.

The aunt made a jug of lemonade for the two girls. It was a hot day and the cold drink was very welcome. But Precious was anxious to see the surprise that Nancy had planned for her.

"Please don't keep me waiting any longer," she pleaded.

Nancy smiled. "All right," she said. "Come into my room and I'll show you."

NANCY LED THE WAY into the small room that she occupied at the back of the house. It had a tiny window, so it was quite dark inside.

"Have you got anything that's really important to you?" she asked Precious.

Precious thought for a moment. She had a dress that an aunt had passed on to her. It was a very special dress, with lines of beads sewn into the hem, and she was keeping it for the day when it would fit her. There was that, and then there was a camera that she had been given for her last birthday. Unfortunately it was broken, but one day

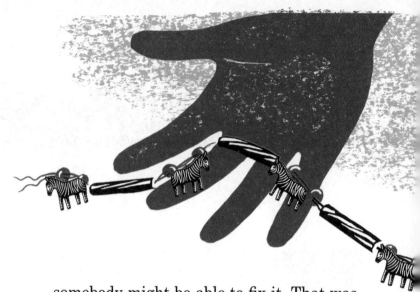

somebody might be able to fix it. That was special too.

"I've got a very nice dress," she replied. "And a camera that doesn't quite work."

Nancy nodded. Then she moved across the room to open the door of a small cupboard beside her bed. Very carefully she took out a cloth that had been used to wrap something up. She unfolded this cloth and took out the contents.

"These are my special things," she said. "I love them very much."

Precious looked down. There on her friend's upturned palms was a necklace

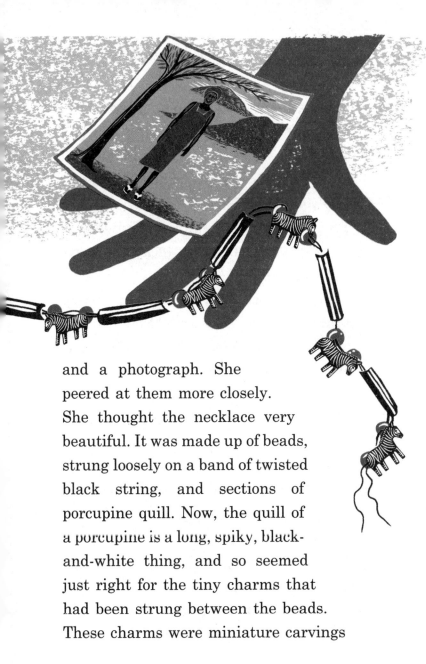

and a photograph. She
peered at them more closely.
She thought the necklace very
beautiful. It was made up of beads,
strung loosely on a band of twisted
black string, and sections of
porcupine quill. Now, the quill of
a porcupine is a long, spiky, black-
and-white thing, and so seemed
just right for the tiny charms that
had been strung between the beads.
These charms were miniature carvings

of zebras, made out of bone perhaps, or of stone that had been stained black and white to match the zebra stripes. It was the most beautiful necklace Precious had ever seen.

"Do you like it?" asked Nancy.

Precious nodded. "I think it's wonderful," she said. "You're very lucky to have something like that."

Nancy seemed pleased that her friend approved of her treasure. "Now look at this," she said, passing on to the other item.

It was a photograph of a woman. The photograph was rather old and had become a bit tattered so that it was rather hard to make out the woman's face. She was standing under a tree, and in the background there was a hill, with another small hill behind it in the distance. That was all there was in the photograph.

Precious looked at her friend, enquiringly. "Who is it?" she asked.

"It's my mother," said Nancy, gazing down at the picture of the woman.

Precious said nothing. There was sadness in Nancy's voice, and Precious understood how she must feel.

Nancy sighed. "That's all I have to remind me of her," she said. "I don't even know her name. I was left all alone when I was very small – I don't remember it at all. I had a small bag with me, they say, and in it was the necklace and this photograph. Somebody said that they had belonged to my mother, and that is what I have always believed."

Precious touched the necklace. The zebra charms were smooth and cold on the tips of her fingers. Then she looked at the photograph again. An idea had come to her.

"Will you lend me the photograph?" she asked.

Nancy hesitated. Then she said, "Will you be very careful with it? Promise?"

"Of course I will," said Precious.

"Why do you want to borrow it?" asked Nancy as she handed it to her friend.

The answer surprised her.

"I thought I might try to find out about her for you," said Precious. "You see, I'm a bit of a

detective, and when there is something that needs to be found out, I like to see if I can help."

Nancy's face broke into a smile. "Will you?" she asked. "Will you find my mother?"

Precious realised that she should not raise the other girl's hopes too much. "I'll do my best," she said. "I can't promise anything, but I shall try."

Nancy handed her the photograph. "Please," she said. "Please do what you can."

At home that evening, Precious showed the photograph to her father. She told him about Nancy and about how the picture and the necklace had been her only possessions when, as a baby, she was taken in by her uncle and aunt. He listened quietly and then, when she had finished the story, he looked very carefully at the photograph.

"This is very interesting," he said. "Yes, this is very interesting indeed."

Precious caught her breath. "Do you know who that lady is?" she asked. She hardly dared hope, but there was always a chance – just a chance – that he might once have met the person in the picture.

He shook his head. "No, I do not know that."

He saw that she was disappointed, and so he continued quickly, "But I do know *where* it was taken."

Precious's eyes widened as she waited for him to tell her.

"It's a very small village on the edge of the

desert," her father went on. "I know those hills, you see. They have a very unusual shape, as you can see in this photo. I went there once as a boy. A cousin of mine lived in that place."

She hardly dared hope. Her voice was quivering with excitement when she spoke. "Does the cousin still live there?"

Her father smiled. "Yes," he said. "She does. She has a farm there. I have seen her cattle when she sends them down here."

Precious asked him to tell her more about the village. "It's a very lonely place," he said. "It's very far from anywhere. Not many people go there."

Precious thought for a moment. Her father had said that not many people went there, but he had not said that *nobody* went there.

"Do you know anybody who might be going there?" she asked.

He scratched his head for a moment.

"Well, as it happens," he said, "I do know a nurse who goes to help in the clinic there quite regularly. She can't drive all the way to the village because the tracks are too narrow and bumpy. But she goes within about four or five miles of it and then walks the rest."

Precious was excited to hear this. "Do you think Nancy and I could go with her?" she said. "We'd be careful."

He looked doubtful. "I don't know, my darling. It's a long way and it's quite wild out there, you know."

"We'd be *very* careful," said Precious. "I promise you."

Obed Ramotswe knew that his daughter was a very responsible girl, and that if she said she would be very careful, then she would be very careful.

"Very well," he said. "You can go. But make sure that Nancy gets permission too."

"I shall," said Precious.

That night as she lay in bed sleep was

slow to come to her. But when it eventually
did, she dreamed a lot. She dreamed that
she was walking through the bush with
Nancy. She dreamed that they were both
in some sort of danger. She tossed and
turned and eventually woke up. The dream
faded quickly, as dreams often do – even
bad ones. But she did remember that she
had felt very frightened, which is how you
usually feel when you are in danger, even if
you don't know or can't remember exactly
what the danger is.

But it did not put her off. Precious was one of the bravest girls in Botswana, and it would take more than a dream to put her off once she had started working on a case. And so she told Nancy about her plan, and went with her friend to obtain permission to go off on their trip with the nurse.

Nancy was allowed to go, especially since her aunt knew the nurse and knew how careful she would be. So the aunt said yes and made several meals for the girls to take with them. There were sandwiches and cake. There were two cans of orange juice and four apples – two for each girl. Armed with these supplies, and with various other bits and pieces that Precious had gathered together, the two girls, accompanied by Obed Ramotswe, went off to meet the nurse at the crossroads where she said she would pick them up. They were both very excited. This was, in fact, the most exciting thing that Precious Ramotswe had ever done in her entire life.

Obed Ramotswe had some parting words for his daughter and her friend: "When you get there," he said, "make sure you go straight to my cousin's place. She'll be expecting you."

"We shall," said Precious. "Don't worry – we'll be perfectly all right."

Her father stayed with them at the crossroads until the nurse drove up in her car. Then he stood there, waving until the car disappeared into a cloud of dust and was gone.

"Be very careful," he said, as he watched them go. But the wind swallowed his words, and nobody could hear them anyway.

THEY LEFT EARLY in the morning. The drive took four hours, but Precious and Nancy both got a bit of sleep as the car bumped its way over the rough roads. At last they reached the place where the road became a narrow track, and, shortly after that, turned into an even narrower path.

"We'll leave the car over there," said the nurse. "That tree will provide some shade for it."

The girls helped the nurse take her bag out of the car and the three of them then began to make their way along the path to the village. It was obviously not used very much, as it was quite overgrown. In some places it had been more or less washed away by heavy rain; in other places, undergrowth had covered it, making it necessary to pick one's way through dense bush and beds of tall reeds.

They had been walking for half an hour or so, making very slow progress, when Nancy suddenly let out a sharp cry of pain. Precious, who was walking behind her, rushed up to see what had happened.

"A really big thorn," wailed Nancy. "I've trodden on a horrid thorn."

Precious bent down to examine her friend's foot. Sure enough, there was a large thorn, broken off on its shaft, embedded in the sole of Nancy's right foot.

"I'll take it out," said Precious. "You lean on my shoulder, close your eyes, and think of something nice. Think of ice cream."

"What flavour?" Nancy sobbed.

But before an answer could be given,

Precious had pulled the thorn out of the foot. "There we are," she said. "All over."

Nancy was relieved, but wanted to take a short rest. The nurse, who had been walking in front of them, must have been unaware of the incident, and there was now no sign of her.

"We'll catch up with her," said Precious. "We can rest for a few minutes until your foot stops hurting."

The two girls sat down on the ground. All around them were the sounds of the African bush: the high-pitched screech of crickets, the strange, lonely calls of the birds, the sigh of the breeze in the leaves of the trees – a sound that seemed a little like that of the sea.

At last Precious said that it was time to go. She did not want the nurse to get too far ahead of them, because if the nurse turned round and saw that they were not there she

would become alarmed.

"We must hurry," said Precious. "Are you able to walk a little bit faster?"

Nancy replied that she was, and so Precious set off at a rather faster pace than before. This, I'm afraid to say, was a mistake, because the faster you walk in the bush, the more likely you are to lose your way. And that is exactly what happened.

Precious was not sure where they went wrong. It may have been immediately after their rest, when they took what they thought was the right path, or it may have been later on, when they followed the course of a dry river bed. Or it may have been when they wandered into a thick clump of trees and had difficulty finding their way

out again. There are a hundred different ways of getting lost in thick bush like that.

After they had been walking for a while, Precious looked down at the ground. Her father had told her about tracking, and how you can tell who has been there before you by reading what is written in the sand. Now, as she looked down, Precious realised that there were no footprints at all – or at least no footprints of a person, and of the nurse in particular. Nobody had walked that way for a long time – nobody, that is, apart from a warthog and her babies, a

small family of antelopes, and, she thought, a baboon or two.

Nancy knew that something was wrong. "Are we lost?" she asked.

Precious looked up at the sky. It is possible to tell what direction you are going in by looking where the sun is. But now, in this unfamiliar place, it seemed to her that they were going back the way they had come, or were even going round in circles.

She answered Nancy's question carefully. She did not want to alarm her friend. "We might be a little bit lost," she said. "I'm not sure. Perhaps we should try calling the nurse. We may not be too far behind her."

They started to call out. They called as loudly as they could, but their voices did not carry very far in that lonely place. Then they shouted out more loudly, and even tried to whistle, but all that greeted their

efforts was silence.

"It's no good," said Precious at last. "I don't think anybody can hear us."

"Then what are we going to do?" asked Nancy in a voice that sounded close to despair.

Precious tried to remember what her father had told her about being lost in the bush. *Try to remember how you got to where you are,* he had said, *then retrace your steps. Go back rather than press on.*

"We could try going back," she said.

"But I don't remember which way we came," Nancy said. "And what will we do when we get to the car – even if we find it. Nobody will be there." She paused. "Can you drive?"

Precious shook her head. "No." And then she remembered another reason why it would not do much good to go back to the car. "And we don't have the key," she added. "You need a key to start the engine, and the nurse has taken it with her."

For a few minutes they stood where they were, looking about them, uncertain what to do. It was mid-afternoon now, and in a couple of hours it would be dark. Neither of them wanted to be lost in the African bush at night. It was perfectly possible that there were lions not far away, or leopards perhaps. Leopards like to hunt in the hours

of darkness, and if they were to meet a leopard ... It was best not to think about what would happen then.

Eventually Precious made up her mind. "We can try to retrace our tracks," she said. "Then, if we find the path again, we can follow it until we come to the village.

They began to walk back the way they had come. It was slow-going, as the ground was hard and dry, and their footprints were not all that obvious. After half an

hour or so, they came to a halt.

"I can't see any footprints now," said Precious. "Can you see anything, Nancy?"

Nancy had been gazing at the ground in search of some sign, but had found nothing. She shook her head sadly. "I think we're still lost," she said. "Maybe even more lost than we were before."

It was while they were standing there, trying in vain to work out where they were, that Precious heard an unexpected sound. Without saying anything, she reached out to touch Nancy's arm. Then, leaning forward, she whispered in her ear, "I think I heard something. Listen."

The two girls strained their ears. They heard the sound of a bird flying up into a tree – the flutter of wings and a high-pitched bird-call. They heard the rustle of the wind in a reed bed behind them. They heard some tiny sounds that could have been anything – ants, even, marching across tiny grains of sand.

Then they heard something quite different.

"There," said Precious. "Did you hear that?"

Nancy nodded. It seemed very unlikely – so unlikely, in fact, as to be impossible. But there it was again. It was somebody singing.

THERE IT WAS AGAIN. And now it was getting closer.

"Somebody's coming," whispered Nancy.

Precious put a finger to her lips in a gesture of silence. She had worked out that the sound was coming from a thicket of trees not far away. She strained her eyes to see any movement, and then suddenly she saw it. Yes, there *was* somebody there, coming out of the shadow of the trees. And it was a boy.

The boy was not very tall. He was carrying a small bow – the sort used to shoot arrows

– and over his shoulder he had slung a bag made of brown animal skin. He was coming straight towards them, and he was singing, quite unaware of their presence.

Precious stepped forward and greeted him in Setswana, which is the language many people speak in Botswana.

The boy stopped in his tracks. Then, in a sudden movement he dropped to his

haunches, whipped an arrow out of the quiver dangling from his belt and pointed the weapon at them.

Precious raised a hand in greeting. "Don't be frightened," she said. "It's just my friend and me. We're lost."

The boy stared at them. He must have realised they meant him no harm, for he straightened up and lowered his bow and arrow. Then, very slowly, he advanced towards them.

"Do you know how to get to the village near here?" Precious asked.

The boy looked at her and frowned.

"The village?" Precious repeated.

Nancy had been watching closely. Now she understood. "He doesn't understand," she said. "He doesn't speak our language."

Suddenly the boy spoke. It sounded

strange to them, as he used speech that was half whistle, half words. It was like hearing a bird speaking.

The moment he opened his mouth, Precious knew: this boy was a member of a group of people called the San. They were people who had lived in and around the Kalahari Desert for a long time. They were expert hunters and knew all there was to know about that dry and beautiful place. But how could she communicate with this boy, who had no idea of who they were or where they were going?

Suddenly it came to her. Tapping the boy lightly on the shoulder, she pointed to the ground beneath their feet. She dropped to her knees and began to draw in the sand. She drew a village, with huts and paths. She drew a cattle pen of the sort she knew villages in that part of the country always had next to them. She drew people standing round the huts.

The boy watched very carefully. Then,

jabbing at the picture with a finger, he said something more. But once again neither Precious nor Nancy could make out what it was.

The boy pointed. He said something they could not make out, using words that meant nothing to them.

"It must be in that direction," said Nancy. "He's showing us."

The boy stood up straight and pointed again. He was looking at Precious as if puzzled as to why she could not understand what he was saying. Then he began to move off, gesturing to them to follow him.

They had wandered further than they had imagined, as they now began a walk that lasted many hours. As the sun began to sink below the horizon, it turned the sky deep red, as if the clouds were on fire. Then, as quickly as the sky had come ablaze, the red turned to dark blue, dotted with tiny points of silver light from thousands and

thousands of stars.

Precious made sure she stayed close to the boy, and that Nancy stayed at her side. She did not want to get lost again. She did not want to be wandering around in a place like this, so far from anywhere, so lonely, so dangerous for any unfortunate creatures on their own.

After a couple of hours, the boy signalled for them to stop. He pointed ahead and gestured to the girls to crouch down behind him.

"What is it?" whispered Nancy, her voice wavering with fear.

"I don't know," answered Precious. "He's seen something."

In the silence of the night, at first it seemed to Precious that the only sound was that of her heart hammering within her. But then another sound caught her attention – the sound of something moving in the bush, something crashing through vegetation.

She sensed immediately that it must be a big creature. Most animals move quite silently, but the bigger ones – elephants, buffalos or rhinos – barge through the undergrowth not caring what they knock down or flatten. The noise she heard definitely came from something big.

She tried to make out shapes in the darkness, but there was no moon, and the stars gave out only a very faint light. She could see the trees, of course, but there was no way of telling what the shapes beneath them were. Until one of them moved – and then she knew. An elephant … Another shape moved. Two elephants.

Precious knew they were in real danger. Elephants do not like people to get too close to them, and if they do so, they will often charge. If you are charged by an elephant, your only hope is that it will decide not to

bother to carry through with its attack. If it does decide to see the charge through, then nothing can save you.

The boy reached for Precious's hand and began to lead her and Nancy very slowly off to one side. They crept along as silently as they could, hoping that the elephants would not hear them, and they might have succeeded had Nancy not trodden on a large twig. Under her weight the twig broke with a crack that sounded as loud as a pistol shot.

There was a flurry of activity from the elephants. This came along

with a trumpeting – a sort of challenge – from one of them. The boy seized Precious by the arm and pulled her behind him. Nancy clung on to Precious's hand, and the three of them ran as fast as they could through a bed of reeds away from the elephants.

It could all have ended very badly, but fortunately it did not. The elephants decided that whatever had made the noise was no threat and had gone away. They resumed their browsing.

The three children continued. Precious and Nancy were now rather tired and were finding it difficult to keep up with the boy, but they knew that they could not lag behind again. For his part, the boy sensed their exhaustion and stopped to dig up the root of a wild plant. Taking a knife from his quiver, he cut it into several parts and offered it to the girls. He gestured to them to eat.

The root tasted delicious, and because it was so moist it quenched their thirst. But it also seemed to give them the energy to continue, and when they set off on their way again they had no difficulty in keeping up with their young guide.

It was deep into the night when they saw a few lights in the distance. These were lamps from the village, and meant that they were safe.

"We've made it," said Precious.

"Yes," said Nancy. "Thanks to our new friend."

People in the village were still awake. Earlier on they had sent out search parties after the nurse had arrived and told them she had become separated from the two girls. These search parties had just returned, only to find that the very people they were looking for had now turned up. Everybody was most relieved.

Obed Ramotswe's cousin was most relieved of all.

"I was very, very worried," he said. "The bush is dangerous at night."

Precious struggled to keep her eyes open. She was extremely tired. "Well, we're here now," she said. "Thanks to this ..."

She turned to point to the boy, but he had vanished.

"There was a boy!" she said.

The cousin nodded. "I saw him," he said. "That was a little San boy. His people live out there. They know how to survive in the bush."

"I didn't have time to thank him," said Precious. "I wanted to tell him how grateful we feel."

"Don't worry," the cousin reassured her. "I think he knows."

They spoke to the nurse. She had spent hours worrying about them and was crying with relief that they had been found. Then they went off with the cousin and his wife to sleep at their house. They were given a small room with two comfortable sleeping mats, and were offered food. They were too tired to eat, though, and dropped straight off to sleep the moment they lay down.

Precious had vivid dreams that night. There were elephants, and shapes that might have been elephants. There were strange birds. There was a little boy with a bow and arrows. There was her father, smiling at her, saying, *You must be more careful, my darling.* And in one of her dreams, an elephant said something to her, but it was in elephant language and she could not understand it. So she simply waved to it and the elephant waved back with its trunk before it became a shadow again and disappeared.

T HE NEXT MORNING they had a large breakfast with the cousin and the cousin's wife and children. The cousin had three children, one of whom was the same age as Precious. They had never met before, even if they were distant cousins, and it was very exciting to discover and meet a new relative. After breakfast, as they sat in front of the house, enjoying the warm morning sun, Nancy told the cousin about how she had come to own the necklace and the photograph.

When she had finished, the cousin's wife

sighed. "That is a very sad story," she said. "Can you show me these things?"

The photograph was passed over, and then the zebra necklace.

"My father said that these hills are near this place," said Precious. "Is that true?"

The cousin's wife peered more closely at the photograph. "Yes," she said, looking up at Precious. "Those are our hills. They are only two or three miles away. Those are definitely our hills."

Precious gave Nancy a nudge. "You see,"

she whispered. "We are in the right place."

Now she asked the really important question. "Do you know who that lady is?" she enquired.

The cousin's wife looked at the photograph again. She passed it on to her husband, who also examined it closely. They both shook their heads, which made the girls' hearts sink.

"I'm afraid not," said the cousin. "We do not know that person."

Precious pointed to the necklace. "That

345

is something that belonged to her," she said. "That was her necklace."

The cousin's wife took the necklace in her hand and felt the smooth carved beads. "Zebras," she muttered. "They are very pretty creatures."

"Have you ever seen it before?" asked Precious.

The cousin's wife shook her head again. But then she said something that made both girls sit up straight. "I haven't seen this particular necklace," said the cousin's wife. "But I know the woman who makes them."

This was a very important clue, and Precious Ramotswe, as a budding detective, was very interested in clues. "Who is this lady?" she asked.

"She lives on the edge of the village," she said. "She is a very old woman now, and she doesn't make these necklaces any more. But this is clearly her work."

Precious turned to Nancy, who was quivering with excitement. "Perhaps that lady will remember your mother," she said.

"I can take you to see her," said the cousin's wife. "I know her well, and she will be very happy to see you. She doesn't get many visitors, you see, and when you don't get many people coming to see you, then there is always a welcome for anyone. "

They found the old woman sitting outside her house. When she saw them approaching, she clapped her hands together, greeting them with a broad smile that was almost entirely toothless.

"You are very welcome, girls," she said.
"Tell me: where have you come from?"

Precious and Nancy told her about
Mochudi, the village in which they both
went to school. As they spoke, the old woman
nodded to show that she liked what she was
hearing. "It sounds like a very fine place,"
she said. "I have never been anywhere else,
but if I ever do go somewhere, then I shall
certainly go to Mochudi."

The cousin now raised the subject of the
necklace. "This girl," she said, gesturing to

Nancy, "has a necklace she would like to show to you."

At a signal from the cousin, Nancy took the zebra necklace out of her pocket and handed it over. The old woman took it, her eyes shining with pleasure. "But I remember this," she exclaimed. "This is the best necklace I ever made. It took me a very long time."

"Do you remember who you sold it to?" Precious asked.

For a moment she feared that the old woman would shake her head and say no, but she did not. Instead there came a very unexpected answer. "Of course I remember," she said. "I made it for my own daughter. I gave it to her because she loved zebras."

There was silence. *I made it for my own daughter ...*

Precious saw that Nancy was shaking. She reached out and took her hand. Then she turned to face the old woman again.

"Do you think she may have given it away?"

The old woman looked indignant. "Of course not. She kept it."

Precious wanted to know a bit more. "What happened to her?" she asked.

The old woman's face clouded over. "It is not a happy story. She went away and was married to a man I never met, because they lived so far away. They had a child – a daughter. They called her Nancy. I never met her either. Then something terrible happened."

They waited. Nancy was looking at the ground; she was not sure she wanted to hear of this terrible thing. But the old woman seemed determined to continue. "They were accused of cattle theft. They went to prison for four years for stealing cattle. The girl went to live with other people, and her mother and father never saw her again. The girl was looked after by these kind people, but they moved away

and nobody knew where they had gone. I think the parents were ashamed too and might have thought it better for the girl to be with those people. They were ashamed, you see, about being sent to prison, even though they said they never stole those cattle. And I believed them, by the way." She paused. "You see, I did tell you it was going to be sad."

"And the girl?" Precious asked.

"I have no idea," came the answer.

"I think I know the answer to that," said Nancy.

Precious remained quiet. She had never imagined that this would happen. Nancy had found the answer to her quest – but would she ever have thought that it would be this? Precious looked enquiringly at Nancy, wondering what she would say.

"I am that girl," said Nancy. She did not say this in a loud voice; she spoke softly, but loud enough for the old woman to hear her perfectly well.

The old woman blinked. Then she looked up at the sky, as if she were struggling to find words and might find some up there.

"You are that girl ..." The old woman said, so softly as if to be talking to herself. "You are that girl."

"Yes," said Nancy. "I think I am. That necklace was my mother's. And my name is —"

"Nancy," whispered the old woman.

"Yes."

The old woman let out a wail of joy. Then, rather unsteady on her feet, she stood up and folded Nancy in her arms. "You are my granddaughter," she whispered. "And now you have come to me."

The old woman began to cry — not tears of sorrow, but tears of joy. Nancy cried too — the same sort of tears that were being shed by her grandmother. For we do not only cry when we are sad; we can cry when our hearts are so full of joy and happiness that there are no words to show how we feel — and it is left to tears to do that.

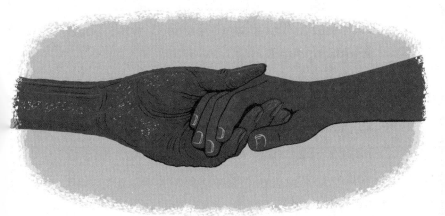

That was not the end of the story of the zebra necklace. Precious had found Nancy's grandmother for her, but the search did not end there. The two girls went home with the nurse the next day. On the way back to the car they stayed very close to one another, of course, as there are some mistakes you do not want to make twice.

The old woman had told them where Nancy's parents now lived. It was not far from Mochudi, and so Precious was able to ask her father to take them there a few days later. Nancy had spoken to the people who looked after her and had told them the full story. They were pleased with what had happened.

"You always have a home with us, you know," they said. "But it is important for you to find your parents, and we are happy that this will now happen. And if you want to live with them, then we shall understand."

Obed Ramotswe drove them there in his truck. It was only half an hour away, along quite a good road, with no bumps – and no elephants either. When they arrived,

Precious said that she would sit in the car with her father while Nancy knocked on the door of the house. But that was not what Nancy wanted.

"You are the one who solved this mystery," she said. "That's why I want you to come with me – and your father too."

So it was that the three of them stood outside the small house that morning and knocked on the door. It was only three knocks – *knock, knock, knock* – but Precious knew that for Nancy knocking on that door was the most important thing she had ever done in her life.

A woman came to the door. She looked surprised to see visitors, and it was obvious that she had no idea who was standing before her. Then a man appeared behind her and peered at the visitors too. Both the man and the woman had kind faces.

Nancy opened her mouth to speak, but she closed it again before any words came. Reaching into a bag she had brought with her, she took out the necklace and held it out before her.

The woman stared at the necklace for a full few minutes. Then her gaze moved up and fell on Nancy. She knew.

In Botswana there is an old custom. If you are very, very happy – not just happy in the ordinary, everyday way, but much happier than that – you show your happiness by making a lovely *wooh* sound. You repeat it – like this: *WOOH! WOOH! WOOH!*

That is the sound the woman made, right

there on the doorstep. Then she rushed
forward and hugged Nancy so tightly that
Precious thought her friend would disappear
altogether. Love can do that, you know – it
can make you disappear. That is because
love can cover everything, including things
that are sad. So love – and kindness – can
cover up hate and unkindness and make
them go away. It can do all of that – and
more.

Everything worked out well for Nancy. Her parents were overjoyed that they had been united again with their daughter, and Nancy, of course, was very happy to have found them. From that day onwards, she stayed with them, although she often spent the weekends, and the occasional weekday, with the kind people who had looked after her all that time. "I am very lucky," she said. "I am a girl with four parents!"

Precious was happy, too. It was one of her best cases, she thought, and later, when she grew up and became one of the best private detectives in Botswana, she always remembered how well it had turned out.

And there is one more thing. To thank Precious for the help she had given them, Nancy and her newly found family gave her a special present. You have probably guessed what it was. Yes, a zebra necklace, specially made by the grandmother. It was beautifully crafted, of course, as is anything that is made with love.